Emergence

A Superhero Novel

Adam J. Ridley

Blake Allwood Publishing

Printed in the United States of America
Box Elder, SD

First Printing: May 2023

Blake Allwood Publishing

Ebook ISBN: 978-1-956727-48-7
Paperback ISBN: 978-1-956727-49-4
Library of Congress Control Number: 2023908627

Content Warnings

Bullying
Depression
Kidnapping
Overcoming pedophilia
PTSD
Sex trafficking
Surviving child sexual abuse
Violence

Join Adam's email list to get advance notice of new books and receive his occasional newsletter:

www.adamjridley.com

MM Romance
By Blake Allwood

Transitions Series
Aiden Inspired
Suzie Empowered (MF Romance)
Bobby Transformed

Chance Series
Love By Chance
Another Chance <u>With</u> Love
Taking A Chance <u>For</u> Love

Romantic Series
Romantic Renovations (1)
Romantic Rescue (2)
Romantic Recon (3)

Melody Series
Melody of the Heart
Melody of the Snow

Road to Rocktoberfest Anthology
Changing His Tune - 2022

Coming Home Series (2023)
A Long Way Home
Family Home
Discovering Home
Finding Home
Bound For Home
…and many more

Novellas
Tenacious
Moon's Place

Romantic Fantasy
By Adam J. Ridley

Big Bend Series
Love's Legacy (1)
Love's Heirloom (2)
Love's Bequest (3)

The Witch Brothers Series
Emerald Earth (1)
Diamond Air (2)
Ruby Fire (3)
Sapphire Water (4)

Acknowledgments

Special thanks to the following amazing people who helped me get this book finished and into your hands.

Jo Bird: Editor

Renee Mizar: Editor

Ann Attwood: Proofreader

And of course, a big thank you to my husband who puts up with my endless stories and handles the formatting and final publishing of all my books.

Part One

Super College: Want it or Not

Chapter One

Prologue - Kaden

THE DANK SMELL OF the rotting building mixed with the cries of the kids around me had become so routine I barely noticed it.

Briggs, the hulking man in charge of keeping us compliant, had just left, and my nose was bleeding. He didn't usually hit me in the face, the clients didn't like it when our faces were messed up, but the drugs they used on us didn't seem to work on me.

Besides, the men who came into my room weren't looking for kids. I was too big. The men who came into my room wanted to hurt me. That's what they got off on.

So, instead of using drugs, Briggs used his fists. No one cared much any longer where he hit me.

I crawled into the corner—the same corner I occupied most of the time. We'd been here longer than any other place we'd stopped at. I'd heard them say something about local law enforcement being friendly.

That was their way of saying they were clients—or at least some of them were. It was no surprise. Cops, judges, politicians, wealthy and poor who liked to... to use kids.

The door opened, and I cringed. I didn't mind the beatings as much as I minded the clients. It was too soon for Briggs to beat me again, so I started to prepare myself mentally for the inevitable.

To my relief, Briggs stepped in. But to my horror, in front of him was a young girl, maybe five or six years old. It was hard to tell since the shadows in this room were so heavy. The only light came from the small window that faced away from the sun.

"You'll stay here," Briggs said, pushing her inside. She fell to the floor crying silent tears. She wasn't new here. The new ones screamed.

Without acknowledging me, Briggs left, slamming the door behind him.

I scooted closer to her and asked her name. She didn't reply, just lay on the floor crying those silent tears. Finally, I moved back and leaned against the wall. Strangely, it felt good to have company even if she didn't talk.

I figured if she were here, her fate wasn't good. Only one kid had been put with me in all the time I'd been in use, as Briggs put it. It was when I'd first arrived. I was eleven. The guard, the one before Briggs, called him the trainer. He was probably seventeen or eighteen, and when the drugs didn't work on me, they used the boy to prepare me, as they'd put it. He'd beaten me daily as well as subjecting me to other, more horrible things.

I'd lost count of the days and years I'd been here, but I guessed I was somewhere around the same age as the trainer had been. I assumed they thought I'd do the same to this girl.

They were wrong. I had fought them since I first arrived. I'd fought, and even though I'd mostly lost, I'd won a few times. I swore as I looked at the dark bundle in front of me that I'd win this time too.

Briggs starved us for two days. No food or water. The girl didn't move for a full day. She just lay in a heap and cried. Finally, sometime while I'd slept, she'd gotten up and curled into a ball opposite me.

We didn't speak.

Briggs came back at the end of the second night. I could smell food outside the door, but I'd been hungry before, and this was a regular tactic of theirs. Starvation often broke the other kids, causing them to do what our captors wanted.

Briggs told me what I had to do to get the food. As soon as he gave me the gruesome directions, the girl whimpered.

"No!" I said, waiting for the inevitable.

I didn't have to wait long. He grabbed me, flinging me across the room. "You'll do it, or I'll kill you."

"No!"

Briggs stood staring at me. "Then, I'll kill her."

Something snapped inside me. Something different. A feeling I'd never experienced before.

I was not going to let him kill her.

I stood up, blocking Briggs's path to the girl.

He laughed mercilessly. "So, the prat wishes to be a hero then?" he said.

As he lunged for me, time slowed down like in the movies I used to watch before they'd taken me.

I felt the heat in my stomach build, filling every part of my body. Finally, when I felt like I was about to explode, I thrust my hands toward Briggs and opened my mouth.

I didn't understand. Dark light? Darkness and light erupted from me. The second it hit Briggs, he turned to ash. I turned, and the same energy that had burned Briggs incinerated the door.

I couldn't remember much about that night. Just that I was able to distinguish between the adults and the kids. When the police finally arrived, we were all sitting outside under a tree, and the building was on fire. All the adults—our captors and their clients—were dead, and the old building we'd been kept in was burning in front of us.

That was the night my powers became apparent.

That was the day the world learned to fear me.

Chapter Two

Lysander

"LYSANDER HONEY, COME ON, you're going to be late," Mom yelled up the stairs.

"Late for what? Sidekick school?" I muttered under my breath.

"Lysander!"

"Okay, Mom! Give me a minute. I'm trying to pack all my frigging stuff."

"Stop sassing me and get your butt down here. Don't make me come up there."

That made me chuckle. She always talked like she was this tough mom, but the truth was she was a big fluffy marshmallow.

I tossed the last of my belongings into the enormous military bag I'd inherited from Pete, my dad's best friend. Supposedly, it had belonged to my dad. But I thought Pete was lying, since the fact that he'd removed the nametags gave his deception away.

No matter. I had barely known my dad; just had vague memories of a man that were more than likely only triggered by pictures I'd seen, and things people had told me.

Pete and Dad had served in Afghanistan together. Dad had died. Pete came home. Since then, he'd been a surrogate dad to me. In fact, he was more than a dad. Friendship was more like what I felt for him.

I came down the stairs and right into Mom's arms. "Oh, baby," she said, wiping her eyes. "I can't believe you're all grown up."

Pete put his hand on Mom's shoulder. "Libby, it's okay."

She wiped her eyes and stepped back. Pete smiled and embraced me just as hard as Mom did. He liked acting strong and powerful, but I knew he was just as mushy inside as Mom.

Pete grabbed the huge green canvas bag, Mom grabbed the box of books I'd decided I couldn't live without, and I grabbed the box that held my most prized belongings. There was a picture of Lowen, the first hero to acquire her powers, and two love letters Mom had given me when I graduated from high school. The first was the letter Dad wrote to her when he first went overseas. The second was the last letter she had received from him. She said both letters were more about his love for me than her, so I should have them.

I had a few other odds and ends. My grandpa's watch, which he'd given me before passing away, and my best friend Lambert's flyball I caught in the outfield, causing his team to lose, among them.

I stuffed the box into the trunk along with my other things and climbed into Pete's old sedan.

Parents without powers weren't allowed to enter the school, and neither Mom nor Pete had shown any propensity for special abilities. Usually, these things tended to be hereditary, so we all assumed mine came from Dad. Of course, we'd never know for sure. Pete said Dad was very talented at getting into trouble, and of course, he'd been particularly talented at drinking his buddy's beers when they weren't looking. Other than that, there was no indication he'd been special.

"Do you have everything, honey?" Mom asked, pulling me out of my thoughts.

"Yeah, if I don't, you can send me the rest."

Mom sighed. "You know you don't have to go to that school."

"Mom, we've discussed this."

"I know, but I thought I'd just say it one more time."

"Mom, if I don't, they'll take away my powers. You know I don't have a choice."

She shrugged and pretended to give up. It wasn't like I hadn't heard the arguments before. Unfortunately, my powers weren't strong. I'd been one of the only black kids in school, not to mention I was also short and a bit of a science geek. Luckily, I didn't have a lot of bullies, but I did have one. The only reason I knew my powers existed was because my bully, Jeff Jones, had acquired the ability to electrocute people and decided to zap me while I was in the bathroom.

I had just zipped up when I heard the door open, and turned to see Jeff. He lifted his hateful little finger and pointed it at my crotch. Fear of what his electrical abilities would do to my junk caused me to absorb his zap. He tried zapping me three more times, and I absorbed his attack each time.

Jeff was without powers for the rest of the day. Of course, he beat the crap out of me after school, but I'd learned I could absorb powers. What good did that do me?

Absolutely none. I couldn't turn his power back on him. I couldn't even keep him from beating me up. So, I decided to head to Colorado's super college and learn how to use what little skill I had, even if it meant I'd end up as some more powerful and arrogant asshole's sidekick.

We pulled up at the bright modern building called *Lowen Depot*. Mom and Pete helped me carry my luggage, and we were met at the entrance. A handsome older man smiled and took our things. One second, we were looking at my stuff, and the next, it was wrapped in plastic, so it didn't get separated, and loaded onto the conveyer belt behind us.

"How...? How did...?" Before Pete could finish the question, I pointed to the sign above the conveyer belt that said, *Superpower training awaits you!*

Pete swallowed hard and nodded. He and Mom were out of their element, and I was, too. For the most part, people with special powers didn't let them possess their daily lives. Jeff had been an exception, but after my zapping incident, he'd been suspended from school after crossing the line with the principal's daughter. Last I heard, he'd been sent to Juvie, where I figured he'd probably have his powers removed, at least.

Pete hugged me, then stepped aside, letting Mom embrace me again. She cried silently, and I considered for a moment telling them I'd rather stay closer to home. Finally, she let go, and I could see the resolve on her face. She had accepted my decision.

"I love you, Mom," I whispered so only she could hear.

"I love you too, baby," she said, and hugged me again before turning and heading out the door with Pete.

I watched the two of them leave and felt my heart ache. Mom and Pete had always been part of my life. *Why am I doing this?* I thought to myself.

I shook my head because something felt important about what I was doing. I might be overthinking it, but I felt a drive in me that said I might be the thing that saved us from total annihilation. I needed to know if that was true or just my fantasy. I needed to learn what, if anything, the pitiful powers I possessed could do.

Chapter Three

Kaden

"**T**ELL ME AGAIN HOW this isn't me going to prison?" I asked my counselor, who was becoming increasingly annoyed with me the longer we worked together.

He let out a long-suffering sigh. "Kaden, you killed at least thirty men. We can't be certain how many. You can't just be put back on the streets when you possess that kind of power."

"So, take the power away, and fuck, I don't understand what the problem is. The SOBs were raping kids. They raped me!"

"And, if you didn't have powers that you and I both know can't be taken away for some reason, then you'd probably be let off the hook, maybe even regarded as a hero."

I slumped back in the uncomfortable straight-back chair he kept in his office. Before being taken, I'd had therapists, and their furniture was usually comfortable with offices designed to embrace you and make you feel better about spilling your guts.

This was not that kind of therapist's office.

"I don't understand why they couldn't take my powers. The man from the school said it had always worked before. Why do I have to suffer with, well fuck, whatever this is?"

Mr. Forsyth shrugged. "As I and multiple others have explained numerous times, no one knows."

It was my turn to sigh.

The professor had come into my holding cell at what they called a group home, and when I signed the document saying they could take my powers, he began trying to exorcise my demons. He tried a dozen times before he gave up. Apparently, my powers refused to budge.

"So, I'm being forced to go to college?" I'd asked the question repeatedly too, but the truth was, I barely had an elementary school education since I'd been taken before I finished sixth grade. How was I going to survive in a college setting?

I'd been in the prison, designed as a group home, for almost a year. I'd been tested, prodded, poked, and asked billions of questions, mostly the same ones over and over. There wasn't much to tell. I kept trying to explain Briggs was gonna hurt the kid, but something had snapped, and I protected her.

I hadn't even tried to use the powers again, at least not on my own. They sometimes made me try things to document that the powers were still there, but I hadn't done anything with them since that night. Yet, the common theme among all the adults I'd encountered since was fear and a sense of dread.

I'd apparently lived more than five years with men doing horrible, unspeakable things to me, and I never reacted when they hurt me, didn't even think I could, until they threatened the girl, but they feared me. Not the monsters who got what they deserved. *They feared me*. I was about to turn eighteen, and all these grown-ups feared me.

I banged my hand against the armrest of the chair. "This sucks!" I exclaimed.

I'd tried explaining how I really felt about the isolation and blame in previous sessions, but that got me nowhere. Mr. Forsyth wasn't that kind of counselor. He probably wasn't even a real therapist.

"Your transport will be here first thing tomorrow morning, Kaden. You have to be transported by bus, and I will accompany you. I should warn you, there will be armed guards along the route as well as, um, specialists who will be with us to keep you... secure," he muttered.

I could see by his expression that he was afraid. Usually he hid it well, but I figured they were on high alert and probably thought I was going to try to escape. Fuck him. Fuck them all! I had nowhere to run to. I'd only hurt those who hurt kids.

Oh well, there was no point in defending myself. My only hope was that once I was at the school, where there were more students with similar abilities, I'd have someone who could at least relate.

Chapter Four

Lysander

"**L**ADIES, GENTLEMEN, SETTLE DOWN, please. Let's get started," the woman at the podium said into the microphone.

We were all gathered in a huge gymnasium. The woman behind the microphone was tall and extremely skinny. It was almost like looking at a pole with glasses and a lot of intensely controlled hair wrapped tightly in a bun. I immediately thought of the old movies about some kid on a prairie that I'd watched when I was a kid.

"Thank you. I'm Dr. Grace Bisbee, the dean of student services. In a moment, you'll be introduced to our president, Dr. Aynesworth. We know you must all have a million questions, and we will, of course, answer all of them during your orientation week. After this morning's discussion, you'll be assigned groups alphabetically by your last names."

A noise blasted behind me, quickly followed by snickering.

Dr. Bisbee looked cross, looking toward what I figured was another teacher who waved his hand palm down like he was throwing a net out to sea. Immediately an oppressive cloud lay over all of us.

"You've been asked to refrain from using your powers. You'll notice they won't work now. Mr. Burns will lift the cloud before we leave this morning's session, but please note we are very serious about the rules regarding using your power. If you ignore the rules, the consequences will be swift and immediate."

Dr. Bisbee was staring at some jock-looking guy a few rows behind me. He was blushing deeply, and the entire room had turned to see his reaction. When he didn't respond, Dr. Bisbee continued.

"As I was saying, we will begin orientation today. Powers are to be restrained until you start classes to allow us to evaluate your skill, willpower, control, and fortitude. We will also begin classifying you based on skills this week."

Just then, a large man, nearly as tall as Dr. Bisbee, walked in. When the dean saw him, she nodded. "Okay, I will turn the floor over to Dr. Aynesworth, our school president."

We clapped halfheartedly, but with the cloud of oppression hanging over us, I was guessing we were all afraid not to.

"Good, good," Dr. Aynesworth said.

For a moment it looked like he was focused on the cloud. Then he looked at the jock and shook his head before smiling again.

"Welcome, students, to Erudo College for the Science of Superpowers. As I'm sure Dr. Bisbee has explained, we will begin orientation as soon as this session ends. Before we start, I wish to speak to you directly about what sort of school this is."

The president scanned the crowd before beginning, almost like he was willing all of us to pay attention.

"First, we are nothing like what you've heard. Erudo College and all the power schools spread across the country operate with some level of secrecy. That is to protect you as students. So, that means over ninety percent of what you've heard is wrong. As many of you are still under eighteen, we expect you to follow the same rules and laws that our host country has designated."

He took a moment to look around the room, and his eyes settled on mine. He shook his head, and continued, "Power isn't difficult to understand. Not really. When the first humans began to experience superpowers, there was a belief that the powers were outside the physics of the known universe. That's untrue. We've simply evolved to utilize different elements of physics. But the rules that govern our universe still apply."

I could hear students beginning to squirm, attention already beginning to lapse. Ignoring the short attention spans, Dr. Aynesworth went on, "First, let's dispel the whole notion of superhero versus sidekick. Those are ludicrous notions that will do nothing but keep you from reaching your full potential. We've learned these past sixty years that there are those with exothermic abilities and those with endothermic abilities. The people we think of as superheroes are usually, but not always, exothermic and can convert and utilize energy easily. While people with endothermic skills are generally less flashy. I imagine those of you who possess exothermic abilities have already begun to build the attitude that you are superior to the rest of us."

He chuckled, then added, "Here's another piece of information that will probably dispel that myth. For every person with an energy, there is someone with the exact opposite. Like magnets, you will be attracted to each other. Don't try too hard to resist the attraction. Once you find your pairing, if indeed they are attending our school, you will both be able to utilize your powers much better than those who operate without an energy match or, as we call them, your polarity."

"What about our nemesis?" someone yelled out.

Dr. Aynesworth sighed. "So, we don't know who will choose to do good and who won't. In that way, we're the same as any educational institution. Some of you will use what we teach you to make the world a better place, some won't. But regarding the nemesis theory? There's no proof there is a bad to anyone's good."

"That's not what my mom said," a young woman sitting close to the front said.

"Aah, Miss Beckerman. We are fully aware of your mom's thesis on the subject. You should know, as we discussed before you arrived, that we do not subscribe to that theory here at Erudo. However, we do emphasize what science tells us about the two energy levels I've already mentioned. Without one, there cannot be the other," he said quickly, continuing to ignore the waving hand of the woman who'd challenged him. "As you can see, we are a science school. You will be taught the basic physics of what we know regarding your powers. You will be required to learn all the same elements of science our non-super relations learn in their higher classes."

I heard several moans around me. Luckily, I was always good with science and math, but many of my friends weren't. I could imagine how frustrating it would be to a lot of the students around me.

"So, that's it from me. You can now separate into your different groups. You'll see upperclassmen sitting at tables around the gymnasium. Please go to the table your name corresponds to. And welcome, students. Welcome!"

The entire gym began to erupt with sound, and I turned to find the P table.

I was scanning the crowd when my eyes were drawn downward, where I immediately saw a man sitting surrounded by guards. They looked like *Men in Black* from the 1990s film. The guards weren't what caught my attention, though. The guy was glowing, well, not necessarily glowing like with light. It was more like if all the colors of the spectrum were combined, they'd give off their own glow.

The moment I made eye contact, my body felt like it was lifting off the ground, and I was being pulled into those eyes. I shook my head and looked around to make sure I wasn't really floating. When I saw my two feet were still planted on the ground, I looked back up.

But the moment had passed, and the guy was getting up and moving toward his table. The sensation from a moment before had left me shaky. My insides felt strange, like someone had reached into me and jiggled them all.

I took a deep breath to steady myself before resuming my search. I ended up following the glowing man toward the back of the room. He stopped at the same table as mine for the last names P, Q, and R. The guards still surrounded him.

I walked behind him. Now I was closer, I could feel the energy vibrating off his body. The strange thing was, I came out as gay when I was fourteen, but in the years I'd been out, I'd never got a woody just by walking past a guy.

The energy coming off the man was warmth, life, sex, heat. It was what you'd expect pure blood-pumping attraction to feel like. It was an uncomfortable feeling like that in a crowd of people. I looked at his back, but he didn't notice me. I quickly scanned the room to see if anyone else was affected by him the same way I was.

It didn't seem like anyone else was about to cream their pants just by being in the man's presence. So, I sighed, did what I could to pull myself together, and moved toward the other side of the PQR table from him, to register for orientation.

Chapter Five

Kaden

I T FELT LIKE I was a heat-seeking missile, and he was my target. I couldn't keep from staring at the back of his head. He had long dark hair that has been combed so it stood high on his head. Besides that, I couldn't tell much more about him, just that something about him set every nerve in my body on edge, no, not edge. It set them on fire.

I had barely paid attention to the speakers until some teacher cast a spell on the students. It didn't affect me, but I could sense it. I could tell what it was meant to do. It was pretty cool, and I wondered why I didn't have that kind of power.

I'd first noticed the guy when I came in, but when he turned around to check out some blond dude who'd magically sent a Coke can flying into a nearby wall, the electricity soared through me.

I couldn't tell whether it was attraction or a desire to destroy him. Maybe it was both. When he turned around, and I could see his profile, I knew he was attractive. Not a jock or anything like that. No, he was smooth and sexy, not rough. Not someone I'd have said was my type or anything, but something about him was different.

I didn't know. It was a confusing feeling that I was still wrestling with when the talk ended. When he stood up and turned around, he immediately locked eyes with me.

It was weird. The same feeling I felt when Briggs threatened to hurt the girl began to build inside me. But it was different, not as angry, not as inevitable as that'd been, but just as unnerving.

He must be a bad guy. That was all I could fathom since I only reacted that way to bad guys, right? Why didn't he feel like a bad guy, then? He quickly looked away, and when he did, it was like the spell had broken. I was able to get up and turn away from him.

I followed the guards still surrounding me and went to my table to find out where I was supposed to go next. I felt rather than saw the guy walking behind me. It was almost as if I could see him in my mind. I could probably even identify the people standing around him.

What was it the woman had asked the dean, something about a nemesis? Clearly, that was what was going on. This man must be my nemesis. I quickly made a mental note to keep an eye on him, and since I could see him wherever he went, even when I wasn't looking at him, that would make the chore easier.

Chapter Six

Lysander

A N EARLY SNOWSTORM SWEPT through the area. No surprise, considering Erudo College sat astride the Continental Divide in the Colorado Rocky Mountains. The staff usually kept the snow at bay, or so we'd been told, but they traditionally allowed the first snow to cover the school grounds for luck.

Orientation sucked in the way orientations always sucked. They covered boring, mindless things the faculty deemed imperative for us to know. Things like using our powers against one another and causing harm would equal expulsion, and knowing when and where to locate your student advocate. I assumed it was the same stuff every school freshman had to learn.

The darkling, as I'd begun calling him, had disappeared after our first day. We each had our orientation group assigned to us, and he and I weren't in the same group. I rarely ever saw him after that.

Remembering the guards who flanked him, I wondered if he was some sort of villain. The dark glow around him would certainly point to that. I guessed maybe I was lucky he didn't try to hurt me.

I resolved to avoid him at all costs. I knew my power was weak, since that was why I'd come here--to learn how or what it was capable of doing. But looking at that man that day, I knew if he wanted to, he could probably rip me to shreds with no effort.

I shuddered at the thought and quickly scanned the grounds for him again. I wasn't sure why he bothered me so much. It wasn't like almost everyone on campus couldn't destroy me in as many different ways as there were people. I was in school with some of the most dangerous people on Earth, yet, it just felt like a regular school.

Whomp! Damn, the snowball hit me square in the chest. I turned around to see Kaylee and her twin brother, Kyle. Kaylee, who'd thrown the snowball, was laughing her ass off.

"No fair, Kaylee," I yelled as I bent down to make my own. Both Kaylee and Kyle shared the same sort of power. They could move objects with their minds. Clearly, that included snowballs.

I was majorly outgunned, and after throwing my first and only snowball, I quickly scampered into the nearby student lounge and watched through the window as the twins took on all the other students.

I couldn't help but laugh out loud. The twins had befriended me on the first day of school, and we'd gotten close fast. Kaylee was the one always setting up practical jokes, but Kyle was often the one who followed through with them. Luckily, it was always in fun.

It was Kyle who'd tossed the can on the first day of school, and he'd ended up getting a lecture from Dr. Bisbee about when it was acceptable to use his powers. Now that I knew his sister, I was sure she'd put him up to it, and more likely than not, she'd escaped the lecture completely.

I was laughing loudly at the soccer team, who were all taking snowball shots at a bunch of students who were probably like me and had more passive powers, the kind the school called endothermic. Kaylee and Kyle, definitely defenders of the underdog, caused an avalanche of snow to slide from the roof of the nearby building and all but bury the team. Luckily, they crawled out, and everyone was laughing at their antics.

I felt rather than saw my darkling standing behind me. I'd resolved to avoid him. *Damn*, I thought, *That wouldn't be possible now*. I slowly turned around, my heartbeat picking up speed.

He was standing so close I had to look up into his face. He was scowling at me. I wasn't sure why, but his angry expression didn't scare me, not like I'd been scared by bullies in high school. Instead, his expression sent a tingle up my spine, and I swallowed hard.

"You think it's funny that those kids are being picked on?" he asked.

I had to think for a moment. What was he talking about? Of course, in my defense, being this close to him, being able to feel his power radiating off him, not to mention being able to smell his scent—soap mixed with pure testosterone—it was no surprise my brain wasn't working.

"Huh?" I asked.

He pointed angrily out the window. "You're laughing at a bunch of kids being beaten up with snow?"

I looked back out the window behind me, and seeing Kaylee and Kyle laughing along with the entire group, I shook my head. "No."

I turned around to explain they were all having fun, but he'd disappeared. The absence of his energy left me feeling strange, weird, and deserted. The man confused me, but unlike the first time I'd seen him, I wasn't afraid. No, I was drawn to him.

I tried to see where he'd gone, and although I couldn't see him any longer, I knew he'd headed back toward the dorms. I thought about following him, but there was no purpose. What was I going to do, force him to like me?

I laughed. I wouldn't be forcing anyone to do anything. The one thing I'd learned in the week since school started was that I was probably the weakest student here. My powers did nothing other than slow someone down. I could only absorb the smallest fragments of power.

Luckily, exothermic students like Kaylee and Kyle were cool and let me hang with them. If it wasn't for them and other kids like them, I was sure my days at the college would be numbered.

Chapter Seven

Kaden

DR. AYNESWORTH HAD RELUCTANTLY let me move about without the guards, but only because Dr. Grace Bisbee had pleaded my case. I wasn't sure why she'd taken an interest in me, but luckily she had.

The guards remained on duty at the college, and if I gave "even an inkling of trouble," I'd be put back under guard.

I still didn't understand why I was the bad guy. Oh well, at least I had one advocate, which was significantly more than I'd ever had before. I went to Dr. Bisbee's office after the meeting where I'd been freed from the guards, and she explained that she had been the reason I'd been brought to the school.

"I want you to have a chance to learn the same as any other student, Kaden, but I need to know you won't go off the rails. So, if you have any issues while you're here, you're to come to me directly. Do you agree?" she asked.

I nodded. "Good. Since I've decided to be your student advocate, let's talk about your classes."

As she went through each of the classes I'd have this semester explaining why she'd chosen them for me, I felt a strange sensation like someone was tickling my brain. I quickly dismissed it. I must be getting frustrated with everything going on and all the people who seemed to be controlling my life.

"Mostly, I think it's imperative you learn to control your power. You'll still have to do your 101 classes. Those are required, of course, but you'll also take my Practicum class. That's usually not offered until your sophomore year, but..." she sighed heavily, "...you've got to be able to control things before you blow us all up."

When I looked shocked, she chuckled. "What, you thought I'd mince words? You'll have to get over that. I don't beat around the bush. You have to get full control over your powers, and since none of us can seem to remove them from you, you're going to have to do it on your own."

I nodded, but didn't respond. I didn't trust the woman, or anyone, if I was being honest. But when someone was nice to me, that usually meant they wanted something. So, until I knew what she wanted, I'd be watching Dr. Bisbee closely.

"Oh, since you're going to be my biggest job while you're here, you can call me Grace. We can dispense with the formalities."

That shocked me even more since she clearly valued her power and control. I nodded, although it put my back up even more.

Upon leaving her office, I went back to my room. The snow had accumulated quickly while I was meeting with Dr. Aynesworth and then Dr. Bisbee. Several students were gathering outside, and I could tell a snowball fight was about to start.

I was still unsure about Dr. Grace, and my mind was trying to find her angle as well as avoid the inevitable snowball fight. I quickly dashed into the student lounge, knowing I could go through there to get to the dorm without getting involved.

I hadn't been here without the guards, and my moment of freedom seemed to take control of me, so I dashed to the cafeteria and ordered a hot chocolate.

I knew people didn't get me. Even before I had any powers, I was an outsider. I'd been tossed from home to home before being taken, and I never had any of the creature comforts other kids took for granted.

So, having the chance to enjoy a hot cocoa, well, that was special. Strange and special.

I was beginning to sip the delicious liquid when the man from the first day came into the lounge. I saw him from where I was sitting in the café. I watched as some jocks began to pick on a group of other students. Then I heard him laughing.

His laughter rubbed me the wrong way. Apparently, this guy enjoyed watching people being bullied. The thought turned my stomach, and I couldn't help but think of the men who'd done horrible things to me and the other kids for years.

I ended up throwing the hot chocolate away, my appetite for it completely gone. I was about to leave when I heard him laughing hysterically. I turned to see a couple use their powers to bury the other group.

God, this man was disgusting. He must love to see people picked on.

I walked toward him, almost compelled by a force outside my control. I stood behind him, wanting to call him an ass, but when he turned around, the words stuck in my throat.

He did something strange to my insides. Like I was somehow under his spell. He was definitely my nemesis or something for him to have this kind of control over me.

"You think it's funny those kids are being picked on?" I asked.

When he acted like he didn't know what I was talking about, the flames began to burn inside me.

I pointed out the window. "You're laughing at a bunch of kids being beaten up with snow?"

He turned back toward the events outside, and I knew I wasn't prepared to deal with these kinds of emotions, not yet.

I quickly dashed out of the back of the building, heading toward my dorm. Dr. Grace was right. I needed to learn how to control my powers, 'cause if watching someone being an asshole set me off like this, I was sure I could be dangerous.

Chapter Eight

Lysander

I NTRODUCTION TO TELEKINESIS WAS boring. I mean, I was never going to be able to move stuff with my brain. Kyle and Kelsey, however, were so wrapped up in what was being taught you'd think it was the most interesting lecture ever given.

Of course, they were allowed to use their powers while those of us who didn't have that skill sat and watched as they performed their magic.

The other classes were the same, but at least they weren't dull lectures about the physics of telekinetic powers. In every class, students with those skills took center stage and demonstrated them to the professors.

I'd been labeled as Terrestrial during orientation. Well, probably before, when the recruiter had assessed me. But I had never heard the word terrestrial to describe powers before I came here.

I watched other students do things that looked a lot like magic. Of course, the only thing I could do was absorb energy, and my professor had warned me not to try without supervision, because if I absorbed too much energy, I could die.

There weren't many people with my skill, but according to the Terrestrial professor, we had a bad habit of doing just that, dying.

So, as the other Terrestrial students created mini storms, transported across the room, and one guy walked through walls, I sat and watched, just like I sat and watched in every stupid class I went to.

Dr. Bisbee approached me during the first week of classes and asked me to attend her sophomore-level Practicum class about controlling abilities. "You're not going to be able to do much with your power until we understand and know its limitations," she'd told me.

Supposedly, her Practicum course was about actively using our powers and understanding their limitations. I had a sneaking suspicion I would be seriously disappointed at how little I could do. Oh well, being able to test myself would be an improvement over simply watching every other student in the school use their power while I did nothing.

The next day I went to my student advisor, Mr. Morehouse. The first-year students were prevented from taking second-year classes "to protect them from getting in trouble," we'd been told.

Mr. Morehouse would have to give me access to Dr. Bisbee's class, and by the time he'd finished what he was doing, I was ten minutes late. We walked in to see a bolt of electricity flowing between two students. One was clearly struggling with the effort, while the other seemed to be enjoying himself immensely.

I was so caught up in the display that I didn't immediately notice the same tingle that alerted me to the darkling's presence in the room. When his presence registered, I turned to see his scowl. Before I knew what was happening, the energy bolt transferred from the students to the darkling. From the darkling, it came rushing toward me, and I acted without thinking, thrusting my hands forward then opening them into an arc. The bolt's power vibrated between my hands before disappearing into my arms and body.

It was as if my body was the ground to the electric charge.

The entire class applauded, but my eyes were locked on one person and one person alone. The one I was convinced had just tried to kill me.

Chapter Nine

Kaden

"**I** WILL NOT WORK with him. In fact, I don't even want to be in the same room," I argued with Dr.Grace.

"I'm not giving you a choice, Kaden. Not only did you involuntarily throw a dangerous bolt of energy at him, but I can tell you have some weird thing going on," she said, motioning with her hands toward me.

"He's my nemesis," I said, mostly because I was frustrated and determined to make her understand how important it was not to make him my lab partner as she had demanded after the class stopped clapping.

"Nonsense," she barked. "That's a myth. There's absolutely no proof that you have a nemesis. Enemies are made, Kaden, not born."

I sulked, not knowing how else to argue my point, but determined to win, nonetheless.

Finally, she sighed. "Listen, Kaden, we don't like to make predictions this early in the game, but the power exchanged between you and Lysander indicates he could be your polarity, your Yin to his Yang."

"Isn't that the same thing?" I asked.

"Gosh, I hope not. Could you imagine the problems we'd have if your enemy was your magnetic opposite? No, son, your polarity is the person on this planet that allows your power to exist. Well, that's another unproven theory. What is proven is polarities help you to become *more* powerful."

She thought for a moment before reaching into her desk and pulling out two magnets. "Look at how these magnets repel each other. No matter what I do, I can't get them to match up as long as they are in opposition to one another. However..." She turned the magnets around, causing them to slam into one another. "...when working together, they are a force almost impossible to overcome."

I sighed. "He makes me feel weird," I finally admitted, knowing I sounded like a child but having no other argument.

She smiled at me. "I'm sure. When I first met my polarity, I was overcome with emotion. Even now, when I'm around him, I feel strange. If Lysander is your polarity, it makes sense that you feel strange around him."

I'd already lost the argument, so I didn't even bother to mention I thought he was a bully. I was still convinced he was an enemy, but as I'd once heard someone say, "Keep your friends close, but your enemies closer."

So, instead of arguing, I just tipped my head in acknowledgment. "Perfect," she said, way too pleased with her win. "Shall we bring Lysander in now, so you can officially meet?"

I didn't even need to answer, because the woman was already on her feet and moving toward the door.

When she opened it, Lysander walked in. I hadn't known his name before, but he looked like it fit well enough. His expression was pinched and angry. I could tell he was as frustrated as I was with the whole lab partner requirement.

"So, you've both agreed."

"I have not," Lysander interrupted Dr. Grace midsentence. "That guy," he said, pointing at me. "...tried to kill me. I will not be his lab partner. In fact, if this goes any further, I will withdraw from school and be done with the entire thing."

He turned to go, and I couldn't help but laugh at his dramatics. It was like watching some old telenovela one of my foster moms used to watch.

The laughter enraged him, and he turned back to me. "How dare you laugh at me." Then he turned to Dr. Grace. "What the hell kind of school is this, a place where you set weaker students up to be murdered by the stronger ones? Fuck if I won't expose this fucking school for what you really are."

He was walking out of the room when he stopped. I could hear something that sounded like singing or maybe chanting. I turned to find the sound coming out of Dr. Grace's mouth. When Lysander turned back around, his eyes were glazed. "Lysander, will you at least stay to discuss this?" she asked, and he nodded.

He sat in the vacant chair on my side of Dr. Grace's desk. "Now that we've calmed down, Kaden, did you try to kill Lysander this morning?"

I shook my head, suddenly afraid of what I was witnessing. "Could you tell him with your voice, Kaden? He won't be able to see your nonverbal communication."

"No," I said, "I didn't try to kill Lysander this morning."

"Good, you see, Lysander, it was a misunderstanding. Now, why don't you go back to your room and sleep on it? You can tell us tomorrow morning whether you've changed your mind."

Lysander stood and nodded, then he walked out the door.

"W-what was that?" I asked.

"That is my ability," she said as if she'd just told me the sky was blue.

"You can control people's minds?"

She nodded. "I don't do it often, and usually only when someone is hysterical. You didn't intentionally want to kill Lysander, but he thought you did. I simply caused him to hesitate before he stormed off campus and lost the right to return."

I didn't say anything, suddenly aware that the tickle I felt every time I came into the office was her meddling with my mind.

"I don't want you to do that to me," I said defensively.

She smiled. "Don't get hysterical, and I won't."

"What if I refuse to work with Lysander?"

"Then you refuse. I don't force people to do my bidding, Kaden, even if they are being a stubborn horse's ass."

I sighed, figuring if she wanted to control me, she could've done what she did to him, but she hadn't—at least, not yet.

"Okay, but I don't like any of this," I admitted. "I don't like Lysander, and he clearly doesn't like me, but I'll do whatever."

"That's a good lad," Dr. Grace said and dismissed me.

For the rest of the day I wondered if Dr. Grace's powers of persuasion had anything to do with my being here. If I were to guess, it was just another way for the powers that be to control me. I wondered how much influence she had over me and decided to do some major studying to figure out what I could do to keep Dr. Grace out of my head.

Chapter Ten

Lysander

PSYCHEDELIC COLORS FLOWED THROUGH my mind. I knew I was angry, but I couldn't figure out what I was angry about or even how to be angry. I woke up back in my room with no idea how I ended up there. I remembered being outside Dr. Bisbee's office. I remembered being upset by that guy. Fucking Kaden.

He'd tried to kill me when I walked into the Practicum class. Mr. Morehouse had immediately taken me out of the classroom to his office. When I blew my top, he just shook his head. He refused to say the guy had attacked me, and after I yelled that I had a classroom full of witnesses, he shrank away from me.

Fuck that! I thought to myself. Mr. Morehouse then escorted me to the Dean of Students office and left me there. I assumed I was going to be apologized to, but that was it. That was all I could remember.

What happened after that? Well, I could guess. I figured someone had drugged me. I had never been high on psychedelic drugs, but I knew enough about them to know that was probably what happened. I was just about to call my mom and tell her and Pete to come get me when there was a knock at my door.

"Who is it?" I asked.

"It's Dr. Bisbee, Lysander, may I come in."

My instincts said no. In fact, my entire being said I should avoid it. "Dr. Bisbee, I'm not feeling well at the moment. Can we speak tomorrow?"

There was a long pause, then she answered that it would be fine.

Strange things were afoot. I didn't know what, but I didn't like it. Instead of calling my mom and Pete, I called the twins.

"Hey, guys, if you're free, do you mind coming to my room?"

"Of course," Kyle said. "Kaylee said we'll bring chips."

I chuckled. I'd only known them for a week, but it was long enough to know they were both human food disposals.

When they'd finally filled up on enough snacks to feed a stadium full of people, I told them what had happened, or at least what I could remember. "The weirdest part," I said, after they'd asked several questions about the incident with the darkling, "...is that I think Dr. Bisbee is somehow involved with drugging me. My senses were on high alert when she came to my door this afternoon."

"What?" Kaylee asked. "She came here to see you?" I nodded. "And? What did she want?"

"I told her I wasn't feeling well and sent her away."

"Smart move," Kyle said, shaking his head. "Yeah, you've got something psycho going on here." Kyle acted like he was trying to stab me.

I didn't laugh, instead I felt concern. "What, you think she wants to stab me?"

"No, dude, have you not seen the movie Psycho?"

"No, my mom's allergic to any movie not made by Disney."

"Oh, that's just wrong," Kyle said, making me smile this time. "We must begin your education now!"

"Anyway," Kaylee broke in before Kyle went off on a tangent. "So, you need to avoid Dr. Weirdo until you know what's going on. Are you going back to that class?"

"I have no idea what to do. I mean, the darkling tried to kill me. I would've assumed Dr. Bisbee was coming to tell me not to come back, or that he was suspended, but now I just don't know."

"Can you withdraw?" Kyle asked.

"I assume so. I don't know why not, since the class isn't required until next year."

"Then do that. You can practice your powers on Kyle and me. We're Telekinetic, which is less intense than Terrestrial. So, you should be fine absorbing us."

I laughed. "I'm not absorbing anyone, Kaylee. I absorb energy, and clearly, not very much. But yeah, we could try it on you two. As long as it's one at a time, you can't gang up on me. I'd prefer not to die after all."

The rest of that evening, we talked about our plans. Mostly about Kyle's favorite old horror flicks and some soccer player jock Kaylee had a crush on. They were exactly what I needed. Friends I could confide in, but didn't turn it into a thing.

The following day, I walked into Mr. Morehouse's office to withdraw from the class. I had another incident where I was put through psychedelic hell. This time when I woke up, I was sitting in Dr. Bisbee's class, right next to the scary darkling himself.

Chapter Eleven

Kaden

"**S**HIT! WHAT THE FUCK?" Lysander jumped out of his seat, knocking his chair over in the process.

I knew he'd been mind-melded again as soon as I came in. He had that same far-off look he'd had the day before when Dr. Grace had zapped him. He was already sitting at the table, so I sat next to him.

I honestly didn't know what to expect, but seconds after I'd settled and pulled up my Practicum textbook on my iPad, he woke up and freaked out.

"Shh, dude!" I said, after jumping almost a foot in the air.

After falling out of his seat, he remained sitting on the floor, staring at me, eyes wide open, like he was about to be killed.

The other students had stopped and were all staring at him. I was feeling self-conscious. "Um, are you just going to sit down there on the ground?"

"Um, are you gonna try to kill me again?" he asked, loud enough for everyone in the classroom to hear. "How the hell did I get in here? Shit, I was drugged again."

"You were not drugged, Mr. Phillips. You were put under mind control to calm you down."

He turned toward the front of the room where Dr. Grace had just come in.

"What, you fucked with my brain?" he asked.

"Language, sir," she reprimanded. "You were irate, so I calmed you, yes."

"Fuck this," he said, standing up and heading for the door.

"Mr. Phillips, if you don't calm down, I will force you to." The threat caused everyone in the room to freeze.

"You have no right," he said quietly.

"Find your seat, Mr. Phillips. We have a lot to cover."

Lysander looked around the room. All the chairs were full except for the one next to me.

I could tell he was afraid. I guessed in his situation, I would be as well. He returned to where his chair sat, picked it up, moved it to the back of the classroom, and sat down.

Dr. Grace clearly wanted to argue, but instead, she shook her head and began the lecture. I didn't trust Lysander Phillips, or, more accurately, how Lysander Phillips made me feel. But I did like that he stood up for himself. That took guts, knowing someone had the power to take control of your mind.

Was Lysander a bad guy? Probably, nothing had convinced me he wasn't. But sure as hell, I was in no doubt Dr. Grace Bisbee was not someone to fuck with.

I turned and found him staring at me. I nodded, hoping to convey I was impressed. Instead, he just scowled at me. Another thing, for sure, Lysander was no fan of mine.

Chapter Twelve

Lysander

I WANTED TO CALL my mom more than ever. I was in a horrible situation. A kid had tried to kill me, and now I was being forced to sit with him in a class I clearly couldn't withdraw from. I thought about going to Dr. Aynesworth, but damn, he would probably go along with Dr. Bisbee, considering she was his second-in-command.

After talking to the twins, I decided against calling my parents. As Nosupes, slang I'd learned since being here that meant people without powers, they had little power against the Supes, those of us who had powers.

Clearly, Dr. Bisbee was powerful, and making enemies of my parents was not the way to go. I needed to make friends with some of the upperclassmen and figure things out, or I needed to get a handle on things differently.

Whatever happened, I wasn't sitting with the darkling. Since I'd met him, his aura had gotten stronger. I wondered why others weren't disturbed by it. It seemed to occupy the entire classroom. Maybe if I hadn't stayed in the back, I wouldn't have seen it as much, but I could feel it regardless.

Unfortunately, Dr. Bisbee must've scared the rest of my classmates because they ignored me like I wasn't there. Oh well, I'd been a wallflower all through my sophomore year of high school. I was used to disappearing. At least now I had the twins who liked me enough to hang out.

Back in high school, when that asshole Jeff Jones had exposed my powers, my friends quickly disappeared. I had to finish school as a pariah. Nosupes were afraid of Supes. That made my days in high school lonely. At least with the twins, I wasn't alone, but I was definitely in trouble. And I hadn't a clue how I was going to get out!

"You could run away," Kyle said.

"And go where?" Kaylee quickly rebutted. "We're literally on the top of the country, and there's a foot of snow in every direction." She glanced at me and waved her hand in my direction. "It's not like he has the powers to stay warm."

That hit me hard. I knew she didn't mean anything by it, but it stung anyway.

"Why is it the woman always has to be the one to figure things out?" she said with a huff.

"Please, when has the woman ever been the one to figure things out?" Kyle asked. I'm sure just a year or two earlier, he'd have finished that statement by sticking his tongue out at her.

"*Hermione Granger*," Kaylee said, as if that justified her "always" statement from before.

"But it's not always the woman," Kyle said, pouting. For the most part, I sat back and let the two go at it. I knew they'd resolve the argument soon enough without my interference.

"Anyway, the woman is solving this one," Kaylee said, and turned her laptop toward us. "Kaden Pierce was found standing guard over thirty kids who'd been part of a sex trafficking ring. From what the article says, he used his superpowers to destroy the men and the building that housed them. There is no definite count of how many people he killed."

"Wow," I said, staring at the article. "So, I'm not the first person he's gone after."

"But those were bad guys. Why did he attack you?" Kyle asked.

"No idea. He may be a bad guy, and he sure gives off creepy vibes. The way he glows with that dark-energy light."

Both twins looked at me strangely. "What do you mean dark-energy light?"

"What, you don't see it?"

They both shook their heads.

"Okay, well, that explains why no one seems as weirded out by him as me. I can see his aura or whatever you call it. It's like this black light. I don't know, it's hard to explain."

"Can you see our auras?" Kyle asked.

"Um, no!" I laughed. "His is the only one I've ever seen."

"Yours would probably be hot pink!" Kaylee teased her brother.

He elbowed her, but smiled. "I do like hot pink."

"You are such a princess," she continued to tease.

Kyle hadn't come out as gay, but my gaydar had pinged when I'd first gotten to know him. He was insanely handsome, tall, blond, with high cheekbones, but not my type. As the twins got back into one of their typical arguments, I reflected on the darkling. Unfortunately, it was him I was attracted to.

Self-destructive much? I chastised myself. I needed to keep reminding myself the sociopath had tried to kill me.

Chapter Thirteen

Kaden

S CHOOL SUCKED. I GUESSED spending years cooped up in a dark room with no human interaction, only to be molested or beaten every time someone did come in, made you forget how much you didn't like school.

I sat through all the first-level classes, watching other students use their talents. I was forbidden to use mine, unless I was in Dr. Grace's class. Even there, the guards I'd been initially assigned would form some sort of magical forcefield around me as I was told to try out my powers.

Since the unfortunate incident where I'd accidentally sent the electric bolt toward Lysander, I hadn't lost control of my powers. He kept his distance and refused to do anything other than sit in the back of the room and watch.

Dr. Grace hadn't asked him to do anything again. I assumed she felt bad for using her powers on him. It was seriously uncool that she had, but I'd never be able to find a way to tell him I thought that. The one time I'd tried to approach him, he cringed like I was about to hit him.

Even after being beaten, I'd never struck back. I wasn't sure why he thought I would hit him, except, yeah, that time I sent electricity barreling toward him.

I still didn't understand why or how that had happened. It was almost like someone else did it. I didn't trust him, and of course, I was sure he had to be a bad person if he made my powers grow inside me, but he didn't deserve an unprovoked attack. I just wished I could apologize.

We'd been in class three weeks when Dr. Grace asked Lysander to try his power.

He ignored her, and I could tell the woman wasn't used to people disobeying her. Finally, she stood up and when she did, so did he.

"You will practice your skills now," she commanded.

Still, he didn't comply. The entire class watched their battle of wills. Dr. Grace's expression changed, and I knew she was putting him back under her control. Lysander, who'd been looking away, turned to face her, and we all watched the silent battle between them.

At some point, blood began to pour from Lysander's nose, yet he didn't flinch. Instead, he continued to stare the professor down. I stood up, remembering the warning made the day of the electrical bolt that it wasn't safe for him to absorb energy above his skill set.

Clearly, he was taking on Dr. Bisbee, and that was bad. He really shouldn't with someone so powerful.

Dr. Bisbee yelled out, "Arrgh," and Lysander collapsed, twitched a few times, then went still.

"Fuck, you've killed him!" I said accusingly.

She looked shocked. "Um, Kathy, go to the infirmary and ask Dr. Wells to come immediately," she said to one of the women sitting next to the door.

"How could you?" I accused.

She began walking toward him, and I immediately stepped between them. "No! Leave him alone. You'll have to kill me too."

I heard some murmurs of assent around the room. Dr. Grace relented, then turned and walked out the door.

Seconds later, the school's physician rushed in, followed by three students pulling a gurney. I assumed they were his interns.

"What happened?" he asked.

"I think Dr. Bisbee killed him."

The doctor looked concerned. "Liam, Kelvin, get him on the gurney. Sandra, see if you can use your powers to stabilize him."

She closed her eyes and began humming. Seconds later, she opened them again, and said, "He's alive, but he's bleeding internally. I've stabilized him, but he'll have to have more done than I can do on my own."

I followed them down the corridor and into the infirmary. Dr. Wells noticed me and asked me to stay in the waiting room. "I'll have Dr. Aynesworth meet you here after we're convinced Mr. Phillips will be okay. I'm sure he'll want a full report from everyone who witnessed the events."

I nodded and sat down with relief. At least Lysander was alive. I seriously thought she'd killed him. I had to admit he was a lot stronger than I thought when I first met him. I was impressed by the way he stood up to Dr. Grace. She shouldn't be using her powers on students who stood against her. She'd been nice to me, and I suspected she was the reason I was here, but she was still a bully.

As I sat in the stark waiting room filled with old, uncomfortable plastic chairs that had been there since the building was built in the sixties or early seventies, I thought about Dr. Grace. Why hadn't she done the same thing to me?

I had often felt the tickle in my head with her presence, but she'd never done to me what she'd done to Lysander. I wondered if it was because my powers were stronger than his.

I assumed she'd feel different about his strength after today. She could've killed him, but he stood up to her. That was more than any other student had done in our class, including me.

Chapter Fourteen

Lysander

I WOKE UP TO the smell of antiseptic and the stark white of the school infirmary. The room was strange, like it hadn't changed since nineteen-sixty-five or something. I only had a moment to wonder why they never upgraded it when I heard talking in the room next to me.

I got up and patted myself down to ensure I had no significant wounds that had landed me here. When all seemed fine and I had no pain to speak of, I assumed I'd just passed out. I walked to the door and peered out.

Dr. Aynesworth was talking to Kaden, not trying to keep his voice soft. "Why didn't anyone try to intervene?"

"I don't think we understood what was going on until it was too late."

Dr. Aynesworth nodded. "You should know that if the allegations prove to be true, Dr. Bisbee will be sent away, and unfortunately, since she was your sponsor and advocate, you too will be required to leave."

Kaden looked at him, clearly surprised by his revelation. "What will happen to me?" he asked.

"You'll be returned to the facility you were at before coming here. They will decide what to do with you from there."

Kaden nodded sadly. "Can I speak with him?" he asked, and nodded toward me.

I could tell Dr. Aynesworth didn't want him to, but he nodded. "After I speak with him, you may do so, then you should pack and prepare to leave."

I returned to the bed, crawled in, and sat in the middle, waiting for Dr. Aynesworth to question me. I wondered if maybe I'd be forced to leave as well.

The president walked in and smiled. "So, I can see you're feeling better."

I nodded but didn't respond. I was waiting for the shoe to drop. Not that I wasn't ready to go, but I would miss Kyle and Kaylee.

"Do you remember what happened?" he asked.

I thought for a moment, trying to remember. My head hurt when I tried. "Um, I have vague memories. I can remember being in class and being asked to participate. I-I um, I didn't want to, or I don't think I did."

I put my hands over my eyes, the light suddenly beginning to hurt them.

"Here, let me," Dr. Aynesworth said, resting his hand on my head, his palm on my forehead. Within seconds my mind cleared, and I could see how it all happened. In fact, I could now see everything, even the times when Dr. Bisbee had me under her mind control.

"Oh, I didn't want to be in that class. I'd tried to withdraw, but Dr. Bisbee forced me to attend. She did some sort of mind control thing on me. So, I was just trying to make it through the class."

"When she tried to force you to participate, you fought back using your powers?" he asked.

When I nodded, he sighed and stood up. "Mr. Phillips, have you covered all the elements in your Elemental class yet?"

I nodded. "Earth, Water, Air, and Fire."

"Have you discussed how all those elements are part of the human body?" he asked, and I shook my head. "This is why we don't put freshmen in second-year classes," he said with a sigh. "Your body contains the four elements. You're mostly carbon which is the Earth. You also have Water, which you know about. You breathe Air, so oxygen and other particles infiltrate your cells and move about your body. But what causes us to function and sparks our lives is Fire or energy."

He searched my face to see if I was still following. Of course, I was, but I didn't have a clue why he was telling me.

"As a Terrestrial power source, you can utilize the energies within you. Unlike the elementals who can only bend those elements to their own will, you can use them." He made eye contact. "You can absorb that energy, all energy forms, and that is extremely rare. There are only a handful of people who have ever had that skill. Some can take people's powers away or negate them, but that's different from absorbing them." He walked over to the window and looked out. "When plants take energy from the sun, photosynthesis, they absorb it. Without getting too technical, let's just say the plant's carbon atoms absorb that energy and turn it into sugar. Well, you know how photosynthesis works, I'm sure."

He came over and sat on the bed next to me. "You absorb energy in a similar way. You can store that energy in the elements in your body, but when that energy exceeds your body's capacity to store it, your cells literally explode inside you. Dr. Bisbee is very powerful. She's also a Terrestrial being, but she's spent decades honing her skill using the different elements so she can cause the neurotransmitters in other people's brains to fire as she wishes. That means she can force you to do things against your will."

"Why is she allowed to do that here?"

He chuckled mercilessly. "She isn't supposed to. Teachers take an oath not to use their powers against the students. However, recently we've had a few students who've made poor choices. We've had to utilize Dr. Bisbee's powers to keep the rest of the students safe. I'm afraid she must've confused what's necessary and what's not." Dr. Aynesworth shook his head. "So, we don't want you using your skills against people more powerful than you again, not until you understand them. Eventually, you'll be able to absorb almost any power, provided you understand the powers and how to store the energies in the elements around you. You don't have to use your own body," he said, chuckling.

I nodded, and he stood to go. "Your friends have told us you are considering withdrawing. I highly recommend you reconsider. Our school has a lot to offer you, and Dr. Bisbee will likely no longer be here to cause you harm. Of course, it's your choice."

I thought for a moment before responding. "Dr. Aynesworth, I've been attacked unacceptably by this school's faculty, not just any faculty, but the dean of students. I will stay, but only if Kaden Pierce is allowed to stay as well."

The president looked at me in shock. "But, son..."

"No, he's not at fault for what happened with Dr. Bisbee. Not only that, but I also read about him saving all those kids. He's a hero, and if this institution treats him like a villain for doing what's right, it isn't the school for me."

His face paled, but I knew I'd somehow struck a chord. I'd believed myself to be an insignificant insect among giants. But he'd just admitted that if my powers were honed well enough, I could potentially render any of these big-bad Supes powerless. Just like I'd done with Jeff Jones in high school. I was quickly beginning to understand my worth.

I didn't mind being kicked out of school. Dr. Bisbee had all but imprisoned me here, and that was enough for me to leave and never look back. But if my abilities were what Dr. Aynesworth said they were, I could probably get accepted into a different school. That meant I might have some play here.

I decided to give it a go and see how much pull I had. If I could make them let Kaden stay, he'd have one person standing up for him. He had done something horrible, killing all those men, but he'd also saved a lot of children who were being used for unimaginable things. The article said he was being contained to prevent him from hurting others.

What about someone supporting him? Those men should've been stopped long before they hurt him or the other children. The fact that the men who'd disappeared had included a judge, a high-ranking policeman, and wealthy businessmen made it clear the real threat was who he'd killed, not that he'd killed them.

"You should reconsider," Dr, Aynesworth said. "Mr. Pearce is a dangerous man. As you well know."

"Maybe, or maybe he was just being controlled."

Dr. Aynesworth shook his head. "No, at least not overtly. Dr. Bisbee can't use her powers on Kaden. It would drive him mad and make him a bigger danger than he already is. If you insist, we won't force him to leave, but..."

I put my hand up, stopping him. "I won't change my mind. Kaden stays, or I go."

The man looked considerably older than he had a moment ago, but he nodded as he stood. "Mr. Pierce would like to have a word with you. Shall I send him in?"

I nodded, and he left. I figured I'd probably made a new enemy, but hell, he obviously didn't have the same vendetta against me as Dr. Bisbee did, or he wouldn't have agreed so readily. That was something, at least.

Chapter Fifteen

Kaden

"WHY DID YOU DO that?" I asked the moment I entered the room.

"Do what?" he asked.

"You know what, why did you force him to let me stay?"

"Because, it's not your fault Dr. Bisbee is a psychopath."

"I thought you hated me."

He thought for a moment. "I never hated you. I didn't understand you. I mean, you have this weird dark glow for one thing. Also, you jumped down my throat for laughing at my friends when they coated the soccer team with snow for being bullies. Oh, and let's not forget the energy bolt."

I cringed. "I didn't mean to do that."

He smiled, which sent strange shivers up and down my spine. "No, I don't suspect you did."

I looked at Lysander, and a sigh escaped him.

"Dr. Bisbee is an expert at forcing people to do things against their will. Did you intentionally send that energy bolt at me?" he asked.

"I don't even remember it happening."

"I didn't remember what happened when she used her dark magic on me either. I'm willing to bet it wasn't you that threw that bolt. I'm guessing it was Dr. Bisbee manipulating someone else to do it."

I hadn't thought of that. Could she have used someone's powers to do that? I mean, it was possible, I guessed. "So, what, we're friends now?"

"If you wanna be, I'd rather be friends than have you staring at me with those angry brooding eyes of yours all the time."

"What?" I asked, then laughed. "Did you just say I have brooding eyes?"

"Dude," he said, standing up and walking toward me. I immediately reached for him, afraid he'd still be weak from his injuries.

He stopped mid-sentence and stared at me. "What are you doing?"

"Supporting you. You had serious injuries."

He looked himself up and down. "Not any longer, apparently."

"That's not necessarily true," Dr. Wells said as he came out of an office not too far from where we stood. "You'll feel fine, because your body is still in stasis. Or something similar to stasis, but it won't last. Take these," he said, handing over a bottle of what I assumed were painkillers.

"When you begin to feel achy, take one. If it gets too bad, call the infirmary, and Sandra can put your body back into stasis. If you don't overexert yourself, you should be back to normal by tomorrow morning."

"Thanks, Doctor."

The older man smiled. "No problem, young man, and good work with your powers. We're all impressed you could hold your own with Dr. Bisbee. She's a tough nut to crack, that one."

Lysander cocked an eyebrow. "Um, she almost killed me."

He nodded. "Aah, but there's the rub. She didn't kill you, and that's the impressive part. Young man, you can take your friend back to his room, but don't leave him alone. He'll need supervision tonight, and I'm sure he'd much rather do that with friends than cooped up in here."

With that, the doctor turned and waved as he walked back into his office.

"Guess I'll be hanging out with you tonight. Or would you rather hang out at my dorm?" I asked.

He coughed. "Um, I think I'll be okay by myself."

"Nope, doctor's orders. Come on. You'll probably feel more comfortable in your own bed. I'll sleep on the floor."

"No, um," he said, his cute face blushing. "If you're gonna stay, I've got an extra bed in my room. I haven't taken it out, 'cause sometimes my friend Kyle sleeps there, and I also use it as a couch."

He was rambling, and it was adorable. I wasn't thinking of him as a bad guy any longer. The truth was, he'd saved my bacon. If I'd been sent back to the holding cell at the group home I'd been in before, I'd have broken. They hated me there.

People here might not like me, but they all had powers. And even though I didn't fit in, I was better off here than I'd ever be there. I shuddered, remembering the metal-lined walls and the impersonal, cold room. In some ways, the dark, smelly room I'd been held captive in was better than that institutional feeling.

Lysander had rescued me from going back there, and I was in his debt. I just hoped I didn't end up regretting that.

Chapter Sixteen

Lysander

KYLE AND KAYLEE CAME over the moment we arrived back in my room. "You okay?" they each asked while warily eyeing Kaden.

"I'm good, but I can't go running around and exercising or anything," I said.

"Like you ever do that," Kaylee said, laughing.

It was true. I was less of an athlete and more a book nerd.

"So, you two haven't met Kaden. Kaden, these two are my friends Kaylee and Kyle. They're twins and argue a lot, but you get used to it."

"Hey," Kaylee and Kyle both said at the same time.

I laughed. "I'm starving. Can you two have Leon order and magic up a pizza from town? I'll pay."

"It freaks the pizza joint out when he does that," Kyle said.

"I'll go get Leon and ask. I think he got in trouble last time," Kaylee said.

I shrugged. Leon was one of those huge bodybuilder guys. I was sure if he hadn't been a Supe, he'd have been a professional football player. Regardless, you could tell he wasn't concerned about getting into trouble. He was also a giant teddy bear of a guy, and Kaylee swooned a little whenever he was around.

That always made me chuckle, and Kyle scrunched up his face. One day when Kaylee went off to talk to Leon, I'd teased Kyle. "He's so…"

"Big!" Kyle finished for me.

I burst out laughing. "You can't pick your sister's crushes, Kyle."

"Yeah, but she dated different guys in high school."

"Well, like it or not, she likes Leon, and he's a nice guy, so buck up. Besides, you've been flirting nonstop with Terry Gilchrest."

"Have not!" he said defensively, but I didn't miss the smile that spread across his face. Not that I could blame him, Terry was cute and sexy in a preppy sort of way. Not my type, of course, but cute, nonetheless.

The pizza arrived in almost no time and we ate in relative silence. I knew the twins were uncomfortable with Kaden, and I should probably send him away so we could chat, but before I could, the aches and pains began to wrack my body. "Damn, that came on fast," I said as I clutched my stomach.

Kaden quickly grabbed my pills; I swallowed one and then curled up on my bed. Unfortunately, the pain didn't subside right away. In fact, I didn't think the pill helped with the pain at all, but it did put me to sleep.

Throughout the night, I dreamed of being locked in mortal combat with Dr. Bisbee. Sometimes it was with our minds, and others it was with old-time swords and battle armor. I woke up twice, and Kaden was there each time, ready to help me to the bathroom and give me the next pill.

Before morning, my dreams shifted from Dr. Bisbee to Kaden. Instead of fighting him, I had my head in his lap. As he held me, he hummed quietly. The sound of his voice calmed me and allowed me to sleep more deeply. Like he was a stronger pain reliever than the one the doctor had given me. As I began to wake, the dreams shifted from sweet to something else... something much more erotic. I slowly unzipped Kaden's pants as he looked down at me with those piercing eyes. I took him out of his shorts and was about to go down on him when I woke. The sun was shining through the windows, Kaden was leaning back against the wall, and just like in the dream, my head was in his lap. He looked... not serene, but that was something I doubted Kaden ever was. However, he didn't look quite as tortured as usual.

I moved, and Kaden immediately stirred. At first, when he looked down at me, he appeared alarmed, almost like he thought I was there to hurt him, but then he quickly got control of himself and smiled.

"You feeling better?" he asked.

"Much, thanks. Um, how did we end up like this?" I asked, not willing to move. I didn't know how to explain my feelings, but everything just felt right.

He smiled. "You were having nightmares all night, and I didn't know how to calm you, so I thought maybe this would help. Did it?" he asked almost shyly.

I nodded. "I was dreaming of battling Bisbee, then I was dreaming of this." *And more,* I thought to myself—*a whole lot more.* I had to get my mind on something else, because my shorts suddenly got a lot tighter.

His smile didn't do much to alleviate my need. "I'm glad. What time do you have class?" he asked.

I looked at my watch. "In an hour." I wanted to whimper, I would love to turn over and do what I'd done in my dream, but something told me this wasn't the time. Kaden was tough and powerful, but he was also vulnerable. He'd allowed himself to be tender with me. He'd even taken care of me. So indulging those fantasies was out of the question right now.

I stood to go shower, and when I looked out the window, I saw several air vehicles sitting outside the school. Then I saw Dr. Bisbee, and the moment I noticed her, she turned toward my window. Somehow she knew I was watching even though I knew we were too far away for her to see me.

"Hey, those are my guards," Kaden said, coming up behind me. "They must be guarding her now."

Three men surrounded Bisbee, and I assumed they were the guards he was speaking of. Within moments my head began to pound, the pressure increasing intensely.

"Fuck! Lysander, what's happening, what's…?" Kaden looked out the window and jumped forward. Within seconds the pain stopped. Kaden was looking at Bisbee.

I was afraid I'd bring on another attack, but I looked anyway. Bisbee was lying on the ground, and the men were bustling around her.

"Did you kill her?" I asked.

"No, luckily I've learned to control my power enough not to hurt people if I don't want to. But I did help her take a little nap," he said, smiling.

I cringed. "Well, I'm not sure what you did, but it couldn't have happened to a more deserving person."

He winked at me. "She won't be bothering you for a while." He looked back out the window. "But I'm guessing she's going to need medical care, not unlike what you received."

Sure enough, Dr. Wells came rushing out seconds later. Instead of bringing Dr. Bisbee back into the school, though, he and his interns loaded her onto the gurney and took her up in one of the large airships. Shortly after, the doors closed, and the ship raced east, taking that horrible woman with them.

Part Two

Bonding

Chapter Seventeen
Kaden

CLASSES DRAGGED ON ALL day, and I was anxious to get back and spend time with Lysander again. I knew I was being an idiot. My instincts got all mixed up when it came to Lysander, but I'd come to accept Dr. Bisbee's theory that he was my polarity. That was why I was so attracted to him. If the magnet analogy was to be believed, it was probably also why he repelled me so hard to begin with. I was just looking at him the wrong way.

Dr. Bisbee's Practicum class had been canceled until further notice, so I walked toward the student hall to see if Lysander was there with his friends, Kyle and Kaylee. It was the same time of day when the faculty had allowed the snow to fall inside the campus, and the infamous snowball fight had occurred.

I thought of it as I rushed toward the hall. The temperature inside the campus was always a perfect seventy-five degrees. Even though we were on top of a mountain, it felt more like we were on a tropical island, or at least that was what I heard one of the other students say.

So, there was no snow today to wade through. Unfortunately, I'd misinterpreted what I'd seen that day. I guessed I'd wanted to see him as a monster, otherwise, I'd have had to admit I was attracted to him.

After all that'd happened to me over the years, I'd decided sex would never be something I'd want to participate in again. I preferred to keep that as far away from me as possible. I also, wrongly, I saw now, assumed if I ever became sexual with another man, I'd do something to kill him.

Last night, as I sat with a sleeping Lysander's head in my lap. I had felt his dreams. I'd also felt when they'd turned sexual. But instead of freaking out or running away, I was enjoying it. That was what shocked me the most.

Lysander wasn't a bad guy, and I guessed I always knew that. He was a regular guy, and I wanted him. I wanted all the sexual stuff with him. I wasn't exactly sure how or why, but the same things the men who'd come into my room time and time again had done to me, I wanted with Lysander, minus the hate and violence.

I guessed the biggest difference was, unlike the evil men, I wanted Lysander. I wanted him sexually. *How strange!*

I was so caught up in my thoughts I almost ran headlong into an upperclassman and her friend coming at me from the opposite direction. The two must've been talking and not paying attention. "Oh, sorry!" I said as I barely dodged one of the women.

"Sorry," she said, and froze when she saw me.

I looked at her funny and then looked around the area, where everyone seemed frozen.

"What's going on?" I asked.

"N-nothing," the girl's friend quickly said. "You have a good day!" She quickly pulled her friend away from me. The crowd began walking again, but no one took their eyes off me.

Weird, I thought, and hurried on my way to see if I could locate Lysander.

I found him standing with his friends next to the soda machines, laughing at something Kyle was saying. When he saw me, I was happy to notice his first response was pleasure. It was quickly replaced with trepidation, but the initial response was good.

"Hey, how are you all?" I asked, trying to sound friendly even though it sounded weird coming out of my mouth.

"Hey," Lysander said. He blushed slightly, and my insides went a little mushy.

I looked at Kyle and Kaylee, who were both giving me the same look the students had out in the quadrangle.

"Okay, so what's up with the weird looks?" I asked, really perturbed.

Lysander smiled and put his hand on mine before looking at his friends. "We've heard rumors about you, or at least your abilities," he said.

"Well, someone should probably fill me in 'cause it's like the entire school is avoiding me and looking at me like these two are," I said, pointing at the twins.

"Is it true that you're a Quadripartite?" Kyle asked and got a punch on the arm from his sister.

"If I knew what that was, I might be able to tell you." I was feeling a bit put out by the conversation. "Who called me that?"

"We heard it in Elemental class," Lysander replied.

"Well, if I am, no one's bothered to tell me." I sighed deeply and said I was going back to my room. "If people treat me like I'm going to melt the school at any moment, I might as well go back to living in the asylum."

As I turned to go, Lysander put his arm on my shoulder. "Don't go. I think it's just a shock. Quadripartites are like unicorns in the Supe world. There have always been theories that they could exist, but no one has ever documented one."

"And how do they know I'm a Quadripartite?" I asked.

Lysander looked at Kyle and Kaylee, and all three shrugged. "Professor Sturgis didn't get into that. We were just told that if it's true, we should all expect changes in the school... for our protection."

"Geez," I said, frustrated. "Maybe I should just go, and who the hell talks about their students behind their backs?"

I was leaving to go pout in my room, a trait I'd perfected over the last year, but Lysander didn't take his hand from my shoulder. "Kaden, we all have powers. Some of us are very powerful, and we learn to control them.

Even if what they're saying or theorizing about you is true, that doesn't mean you can't control your powers."

"What if I can't?"

"Didn't you already?" he asked.

"What do you mean?" I asked, unsure what he was talking about.

"Dr. Possess Your Brain?" he hinted, and I immediately knew what he meant. Smiling, I nodded. "Okay, we all need chocolate. Kyle, Kaylee, either stop looking at him like you've seen the second coming or go away. Kaden needs to feel normal for a minute, not be stared at like an animal in the zoo."

Both siblings sighed, looked at each other, and shrugged.

"If you try to turn us to mush, just know we're gonna dump a building on you."

"Noted, and if you dump a building on me, I'll turn you both into frogs."

All three of them laughed. "You're an Elemental Quadripartite, and you have to be a Terrestrial to turn people into things."

"Well, I'll do something as soon as I can figure out what that is."

After being chastised by Lysander, the twins chilled out, and the tension eased enough for us to sit and enjoy each other's company. I even figured they were enjoying the looks everyone was sending us. I could've done without them, but if people were going to treat me like the ultimate outsider, at least I could have friends to see me through the process.

After supper, we all huddled in Lysander's room. The twins had asked me every question they could think of about my powers, but I was mostly clueless. "I know I can control things, bend them to my will. Before she tried to kill Lysander, Dr. Grace, you know... Bisbee, had me using my powers to cause the weather to change. I could also manipulate stone. She'd tried to have me negotiate Water, but I could only make it blip a bit or ripple, nothing significant."

"What about Fire?" Lysander asked.

I smiled. "I'm particularly good with Fire, and even more accurately, energy. I can cause things to change." He looked at me, and I knew he understood that was how I'd incapacitated the former dean of students. I had felt the injuries inside Lysander. I should've been able to feel his life pulse too, but I'd been too upset to notice at the time of the incident.

However, as I sat in the waiting room while the doctor and his interns worked on Lysander, I could feel where he'd been hurt. It'd been easy, maybe too easy, to return the same injuries to Bisbee when she intentionally attacked Lysander again.

"So, you can control all four elements?" Kyle asked.

I shrugged. "I mean, I guess. But it doesn't feel all that special to me. It's not like I'm moving huge snowbanks and dumping them on the soccer team or anything."

Both Kyle and Kaylee laughed before Kaylee said, "You know, they so had that coming."

We spent the rest of the night teasing each other, the initial shock of my skills having relaxed a bit. I was happy

Lysander and the twins weren't treating me like most others I'd met here or at the group home. I didn't like feeling like an outsider, although I'd always been that. Sometimes, I just wanted to fit in.

I spent the night in Lysander's room again. I felt safe there—safer than I thought I'd felt in a long time.

He didn't complain when I stripped my shirt off and crawled into the bed across from him. I probably should've asked, but I just couldn't. I didn't want him to say no. I'd learned enough about Lysander in the last couple of days to know he was probably too nice to kick me out.

That night I lay awake staring at the dark-covered figure across from me. "You asleep?" he asked.

"No, not yet."

"I'm sorry about yesterday and today. It seems your first few weeks at school have been as bad as mine."

I sighed. "Yeah, but at least no one's tried to kill me yet."

He chuckled. "There's time," he said like it was inevitable.

"Um, Lysander?" I asked and could feel my cheeks burn.

"Yeah?" he asked.

"Can we sleep together?"

There was silence before Lysander got up and turned the lamp on next to his bed.

"Are you sure?" he asked.

I shook my head. "No, it freaks me out that I want to, but last night when your head was in my lap, that's the most peace I've felt in a long time, and I know that makes me weird."

"Shut up. It makes you normal. I'd love to sleep with you, Kaden. But you need to know I want to do a lot more than just cuddle. Are you ready for that?"

"I'm not. I mean, I want to too, but…"

"Your past?" he asked, and I nodded, trying not to cry like the little kid I felt like.

"Then, we'll just cuddle, but you're too big to fit in this little bed, so pull yours over to mine and we'll put them together."

I jumped up and quickly moved the bed until it butted right up to Lysander's, and as soon as I crawled in, he snuggled up against me. My cock immediately hardened.

"Wow, he's glad to see me," Lysander teased.

"He is, but this is really what I need," I said as I pulled him close to my chest.

"Yeah, me too." Lysander turned around and kissed me chastely on the lips. "Tonight, we're gonna cuddle, and then tomorrow we'll figure this out," he said, moving his hand between us.

"Tomorrow we'll figure it out. Got it!" I said happily.

When I was a little kid, I'd stayed with a couple with three Labrador Retrievers. I didn't think I was with them for more than a month, but they had a huge pool in their backyard. The dogs and I would play for hours, jumping in and out of the pool.

Every night after supper, the dogs and I would lie in front of the television as my foster parents watched the news.

Holding Lysander in my arms as I fell blissfully asleep was like I'd felt curled up with the dogs. Like nothing could touch me. Like I was surrounded by love and acceptance.

I wasn't sure if it was because Lysander was my polarity, as Dr. Grace had suggested. But if that was the case, I was really happy he was.

Chapter Eighteen

Lysander

I WONDERED WHETHER BEING in Kaden's presence made me dream, or if it was because I was sleeping lighter than I would've if I'd been alone.

Kaden was sitting in a temple built into one of the mountains surrounding us. He was seated like an old Buddha statue in the lotus position. He was also the size of the ancient Buddhas.

The valley surrounding the temple was clearly rich fertile land and swarms of people were working the fields.

I wondered why he just sat watching instead of interacting. I moved toward the statue, but the closer I got, the more the people seemed to block me. At first it was just one or two people asking me nonsensical questions, but as I pushed forward, the crowds became thicker.

Eventually, people began to shove and push me, becoming more and more aggressive the closer I got.

Finally, I was knocked to the ground. When I looked up, Dr. Bisbee was standing over me, smiling. The pain hit my head instantly, and I screamed.

I woke with a start, Kaden's arms still holding me tight. "Shh, I'll never let them get to you," he said.

I nodded before figuring out what he'd said. "Wait, did you see my dream?"

"Were you in a field with a bunch of jackasses that wouldn't let you get to me?" he asked.

"Yep, that's weird," I said, then quickly sat up. "Wait, did you see my dreams last night too?"

He was silent for so long that I was afraid I'd offended him.

"Wow, so you're peeping on my dreams, are you?" I asked, awake now.

He began to freak out, so I decided to turn things around. I called him a Peeping Tom and began tickling him.

"Oh, no, not cool, no tickling!"

"Yes, it's totally fair!"

"Is that so?" he asked, and easily flipped my small frame on my back and turned the tickling back on me.

I was yelling for him to stop when Kyle burst in! "What the hell's going on?" he asked.

Kaden and I froze and looked at Kyle, who clearly thought he was torturing me.

When we saw his expression, we both burst out laughing. "Oh my God, you should see your face!"

"Shut up. God, I thought you were dying or something." I laughed so hard I was crying. "Dang, I hate you both!" he said and slammed the door.

We rolled into each other as the laughing stopped.

Kaden sat up and smiled. Then he leaned over and kissed me, chaste at first, then when he pulled back, the moment shifted.

He kissed me again, but this time the kiss deepened.

"I really like you," he said, "...but..."

"Kaden," I said, and put my hand on the side of his handsome face. "I'm a virgin. I'm not in a huge hurry, okay? When we're ready, we'll know it."

Kaden smiled at me and kissed me again before slipping his arm back around me and nuzzling me close.

The next morning, I woke up happier than I'd been in a long time. I was concerned Kaden would be upset, considering all he'd been through, but luckily, he was still asleep. I quickly darted into the bathroom and showered. Today was Saturday, and I wanted to pick up groceries from town, since I'd decided if people were going to act like assholes, it'd be better to cook in the dorm. That way, if Kaylee and Kyle wanted to join, it could be the four of us.

When I came out of the bathroom, Kaden sat on the bed, sipping a cup of coffee he'd made while I was in the shower.

"You okay?" I asked as I crawled onto the bed and curled up next to him.

"I'm still a little freaked out, but yeah." He leaned over and kissed the top of my head. "You smell good."

"You do too," I said, and would've been happy to let the morning turn into something more, but I knew he wasn't ready. I needed to give him space. "Anyway, I need coffee too. Do you want to go with me to town? I'm going to go on the airbus this morning for groceries. If you're interested, I thought we could cook more this week. That way you don't have to deal with the looks."

"I'm pretty sure that's not going to be my choice, I'm afraid," he said.

I leaned up and looked at him. "Why do you think that?"

"It's a feeling. After we fell asleep again, the dream continued. I dreamed people were going to block us from seeing each other. Change is coming, Lysander. I think the dream was a warning."

I sighed. "Maybe not. Regardless, let's go shopping, then we can go skiing. It'll be fun."

Kaden smiled, but I knew he wasn't convinced we'd be allowed to go.

Luckily, I'd been right, and we loaded onto the airbus and were transported from the mountaintop to Denver. We quickly stopped at Mom's. I'd called to tell her I was stopping by to pick up my ski gear, so of course, Pete showed up too.

We ended up being asked to stay for lunch. Of course, I immediately felt guilty that poor Kaden was caught in the middle of all the chaos that was Mom and Pete.

"So, you're our boy's sweetheart," Mom said, and I moaned.

"Mom, please," I said, feeling embarrassed for Kaden.

Kaden smiled. "He's special to me," he admitted.

"Where are you from, son?" Pete asked.

"Okay, stop the third degree. We just stopped by to get my skiing equipment and go grocery shopping. I didn't bring him to meet the freaking parents."

Pete and Mom chuckled, and I swear Pete said, "Busted," under his breath.

"Pete, how's it going with your new building projects?" I asked, knowing that was usually a sure way to get him to focus on his favorite subject, construction.

Pete winked at me, telling me he was on to my tricks, but he let up and began talking about all the troubles he was having with his new crew.

The bus was scheduled to leave at six, and we still needed to get to the grocery store, so we said our goodbyes. "He seems sensible." Mom whispered before we left, so Kaden couldn't hear that she liked him.

"And we just started dating. No kidding, Mom, we haven't even been on a date officially. So, don't get your mind fixated on your dream gay wedding!"

She huffed. "You're impossible. Go on and rescue him from Pete. You know by now your godfather is giving him the *Godfather treatment*."

"I should've known better than bringing him here."

"Nonsense, this is our compensation for raising you, dear. We get to harass anyone you bring home. Now run along and remember to call me more. I worry about you."

I chuckled as I put my arm into Kaden's and pulled him out the door. Pete was still telling him a story involving the gory death of someone who'd mistreated his date. I was sure the message was clear enough.

"Sorry," I said to Kaden as the same airbus driver from before picked us up, and whisked us toward the grocery store.

"I think he pretty-much threatened to have me dismembered if I screw with you."

"No doubt. Pete is intense on the best of days."

"They love you," he said, his voice so full of emotion that I turned toward him.

"They do. I'm lucky."

"You have no idea how lucky you are."

"One day, when you feel up to it, I'd like to know how you grew up. I'm guessing it's tough to talk about, but when you're ready," I said.

"One day," was all he said.

We were silent the rest of the way to the store. I knew he needed some time to himself. I wasn't sure how exactly I knew, but when it came to Kaden Pierce, I seemed to know more than I should.

By the time we got back to campus, I was exhausted. In one trip, we brought the groceries and my skiing equipment to my room before crashing onto the two beds that were still pushed together.

Kaden turned to me, and said, "I never knew my parents. For as long as I can remember, I've been moved from home to home. None of them lasted for more than a few months. Then, eventually, I was sold into slavery. The last foster parent I had..."

I listened as he told the story. He was intentionally vague, and I couldn't say I blamed him, but as he told me his history, I could see in my mind's eye what he'd encountered. I could feel the pain and anguish. The feeling of loss that little boy had, then the intense pain and internal judgment after he'd been sexually assaulted.

Even though he only shared a few thoughts, I'd seen it all. I'd *felt* it all.

I didn't cry, although that was what I wanted to do. I wanted to weep for that little boy. I wanted to attack those who'd hurt him. He blocked me from seeing the event when his powers finally came to him, but I could feel the sadness and shame around it.

Eventually, I knew he'd release that information to me, but as I was able to explore his entire youth, I figured the last days of his childhood were just too much to share right now.

That night, after putting things away, we lay in bed watching some ridiculous sitcom about a group of superhero wannabes. The show had been on forever, but the reruns were still hilarious.

Neither of us talked much. The day had been as exhausting for him as it had for me; but it had brought us closer as well. That night we slept soundly, but instead of him holding me, I slept spooned to him the entire night.

Kaden's vulnerability was palpable. How someone could live through all he'd experienced and not be the villain I initially thought he was, was a testament to how strong this incredible man in my arms was.

Chapter Nineteen

Kaden

I DIDN'T MEAN TO share my life story with Lysander. But meeting his family, even the very poorly veiled threats by Pete, his pseudo father, as he'd called himself, had told me how much the man loved him.

I'd never had that kind of love. No one had wanted me for long. Something had always gone wrong. I assumed it would just be a matter of time before Lysander felt the same, but for now, it felt good to have someone who wasn't repulsed by me.

I'd let him in almost completely. Almost. I still couldn't let him in entirely. The events that day, the way I felt as I destroyed the men who'd used me and hurt the other children in such horrific ways.

I was more afraid of him seeing that than anything else he might see in my past. I'd been swept up in my powers that day. They had consumed me. But I had also let them flow, not even trying to restrain myself. I wasn't sure I could have, but that didn't negate the fact that I hadn't tried.

No, I wasn't ready for Lysander to know that about me yet. I probably never would let him know that part of me. I was embarrassed by that person, but a part of me, a very significant part, wouldn't hesitate to do it again. I didn't regret the deaths of those men. In fact, I was pleased they were dead. Pleased the kids I'd rescued might someday have a chance to overcome it. Any chance of that was better than what they'd experienced at the hands of those evil men.

The following day was Sunday, and we got up early. Kaylee and Kyle joined us as we went with a group of mostly upperclassmen and women who were avid skiers.

I had never been skiing, having spent my entire childhood in the deserts of Arizona. I'd never even been to the mountains, so I had to learn on what they called the bunny hill.

Mostly I landed on my ass repeatedly, and we all laughed each time I fell down. I'd never had friends before. I'd never had anyone. But I felt the kinship between the twins, Lysander and myself growing like we were somehow meant to be friends.

I was utterly exhausted that night. We went to the lodge to return my skis and boots. I'd never made it past the bunny hill, but I could tell none of our group cared that much.

When Kyle brought us all cups of hot chocolate, I stared at the drinks, and before I could hide it, I was showing how emotional I was.

"Dude, it's just hot cocoa," Kyle scoffed.

I snorted, then sighed. "You know, I never had hot cocoa until a year ago. So, it probably has more meaning to me than it should."

I kept my head lowered, willing the emotions to stabilize.

Kaylee reached over and put her hand on mine. "We all understand, Kaden. We weren't judging. Kyle's an ass, but even he gets how tough your past must've been for you."

Kyle had just given his sister a hateful look when I looked up. But as his gaze returned to mine, I saw what she said was true. They all seemed able to empathize with me. I smiled, took my hot cocoa in hand, and lifted it. "Here's to new friendships!"

"Hear! Hear!" the group said. We spent the rest of the day teasing each other, and by ten, we were all tired enough to turn in for the night.

That day would go down as one of the best days of my life.

Monday morning, we all headed out for class.

When I got to my first class, the same guards who used to watch over me were waiting at the classroom door.

"Really? Again?" I asked.

"Mr. Pierce, please come with us to the president's office," they said.

I had no choice but to follow. I'd swear this would never end. I knew from experience it did no good to ask them why I was going there. The men were experts at being assholes.

When I arrived, more guards were stationed inside. There was also a man dressed in an out-of-date, pin-striped suit. I was no expert on style or anything, but even I knew that suit went out of style before I was born. He was also half my height, bald on top, and the hair on the side of his head stuck out, giving him a distinctive Albert Einstein look.

"Mr. Pierce, thanks for joining us," Dr. Aynesworth said and gestured toward a chair. I didn't even have the energy to argue that I hadn't been given a choice.

"Let's get right to it. With Dr. Bisbee no longer able to supervise you here at the school, we no longer feel like the school is appropriate." I sat up to argue when the president put his hand up to stop me.

"That said, I've promised Mr. Phillips not to have you removed. But we can't have you in the school without someone who can manage your unique skills if there is ever a need to do so."

Dr. Aynesworth turned toward the man. "Let me introduce you to Dr. Fagan. He was once on our faculty, but retired a few years ago. He's agreed to come out of retirement to assist you in your studies."

I looked at the man. "You mean to keep me under control."

"Precisely," Dr. Aynesworth said without missing a beat.

The older man stared at me, eventually making me squirm. "Do you know how long it would take you to destroy the school?" he asked.

I looked around the room.

"Huh?" I asked.

"Huh," he repeated. "I see you've got lovely manners. We'll work on that, but let me ask you again. Do you know how long it would take you to turn the school and every inhabitant to ash?"

I shook my head. "No, I haven't considered it."

"I doubt that, son. A person with your skill seldom doesn't consider what level of damage he can do at any given moment."

I looked at him, alarmed. I didn't even know how to respond.

He watched me silently. No one moved. "Maybe your powers are too new. When did you first use them?" he asked.

"A year ago?

"So, when you turned the cesspit you were being held in to ash, that was your first time using your powers."

I nodded.

"Then no, you probably haven't considered it. I do not think you are safe here, not yet. But you probably can be." He turned to Dr. Aynesworth. "I recommend Mr. Pierce join me at my cabin in Leadville. We can perfect his skills, and I can hopefully help him adjust to having these powers."

"Wait, I don't want to leave. I've just made friends."

"Good, that's good," the man said. "But if you don't want to incinerate them accidentally, you should spend some time at my cabin. Once we've worked together for a week or so, you should be contained enough that you can have your friends visit. I'm not that far from the school, after all."

I looked around the room. I could tell saying no wasn't an option, but even knowing that, for a second, I considered pushing my luck. "Can I at least say goodbye?" I asked.

"Of course, you can," the man said. His face lit up like a light bulb. "We'll leave after lunch. Meet me back here with your belongings."

"Will I ever see them again?" I asked.

The man's face fell. "Son, you aren't a prisoner. You're just a very powerful Supe. And, of course, you'll see them again. Soon, if I have my way. A man with your power isolated from the world is a dangerous thing. Here's my landline number," he said, handing me a small yellow Post-It with a phone number. "Your friends can call anytime. Your training will be rather lax while you're with me."

He patted me on the back and all but shoved me out of the office.

"What the hell just happened?" I asked under my breath.

"What?" Lysander asked, shocked and clearly frustrated at the news. "How long will you be gone?"

I shrugged. Lysander and the twins had all come after I texted them asking if I could see them before I had to leave. "I wasn't told exactly, just that I would be gone for a while. But I was told, this time at least, I wasn't a prisoner. You can visit me."

Kyle shook his head. "I don't like it. I mean, the school picked Bisbee as the school's protection from you, and she almost killed Ly."

Lysander looked at him and shook his head. "Lysander's my name, Kyle. I don't want a nickname, particularly one which means I can't tell the truth."

Kyle shrugged, and I couldn't help but chuckle at his expression. The abbreviation of his name had begun yesterday, and Lysander was having nothing to do with it. "You need a nickname..."

"No, you need to let it go, and we need to focus on the issue at hand," Kaylee said. Of course, that ended up settling the conversation. Kyle usually let things go when his sister put her foot down.

"So, do you think you'll be safe?" Kaylee asked.

"I think so. He doesn't push any bad buttons. In fact, he feels like what you'd think a fatherly figure who works at a science school in the mountains might feel like. I think I trust him."

Lysander sighed and cuddled up to me. "We just started dating," he said with a bit of a whine in his voice.

"He gave me his number and said you can call anytime," I said, handing the little yellow Post-It to him.

"Well, if you feel threatened in any way, text us, and we'll do whatever we can to help," Lysander said, his voice stronger. "I know what it feels like to be trapped and not have anywhere to turn. I don't want you stuck in the same situation."

I smiled. Lysander was really concerned. It was another first for me since no one I'd ever known cared whether or not I felt safe. I couldn't remember another human who cared whether I lived or died, but somehow, in just a few weeks, Lysander had truly become someone who did. I looked at Kyle and Kaylee and saw similar expressions. It felt strange. So, this was what caring felt like.

"I will," I said, a little emotional at their concern. "But if he can help me control my powers, it'll be worth it. I'm not sure I've got control of the powers right now, and I don't like having that kind of responsibility."

Lysander held me for a while. His hair still smelled like the shampoo from this morning's shower, and his arms felt amazing as he embraced me.

"I'll call you tonight. Make sure you tell this Dr. Fagan or whatever, that you need to be able to talk tonight, so we don't worry too much."

I leaned down and kissed him. "I'll make sure we can chat."

He peeled away from me and waited for the twins to say their goodbyes.

As I strolled toward the president's office with my pitiful belongings packed up in a small bag on my shoulder, I thought, at least I had one weekend with three people I liked before I lost it all. If my past was any indication, I could see the end of those friendships, even as they were just beginning.

Chapter Twenty

Kaden

I WALKED INTO AN argument between Dr. Fagan and Dr. Aynesworth and heard that Dr. Aynesworth wanted Dr. Fagan to take the guards. He refused just as I walked in.

Dr. Aynesworth looked at Dr. Fagan as if he wanted to argue more, but even I could tell by Dr. Fagan's face, Dr. Aynesworth wasn't going to win.

I followed the little man down the corridor and into a small airship, not much bigger than a car. The vehicle was so small I wondered if I was going to fit. From the look of the vehicle, it was custom-made for the smaller man.

As soon as I was belted in, the airship rushed straight into the air. My stomach did several flips and flops, and I was concerned I would puke. A second later, Dr. Fagan flipped the car into straight-down mode, laughing hysterically.

"God, man, you're gonna kill us!" I yelled.

Just before we crashed nose-first into the mountain, Dr. Fagan leveled out and headed cross-country toward wherever we were going.

"You contain yourself well. I almost thought you'd blow us to smithereens when I caused you to freak out. That's good and shows you have some level of self-control."

"You were testing me?" I asked, confused, and still trying not to puke.

"Oh yes, this first week's tests will be to determine how far you go before you explode."

"Aren't you afraid I'll incinerate you?" I asked. When I looked over, Dr. Fagan was gone, and in his place was water in a Fagan-shaped form.

He reverted to his human form and smiled. "Do you know what would happen if you incinerated me?" he asked.

I stared at him in shock, not responding. "I'd simply turn to steam, then reform back into my body. I'm an Elemental and an old one, so your go-to power isn't going to destroy me, son. But it does sting to be turned to steam, so I'd prefer you to let me know when you're reaching your limits. If you can."

Dr. Fagan chuckled and turned his airship south, pushed the accelerator, and within five minutes, he began to slow down and descend to a forest below us.

Dr. Fagan had said we were going to his cabin, but there was no cabin to be seen. I figured maybe this was another test, so I began preparing myself for whatever was coming my way.

The airship stopped and hovered for several moments before an image of a very large log cabin began to waver into view. "Wow, how did you get that to cloak itself?" I asked, totally in awe.

He smiled at me. "As I told you, I'm an Elemental. I control how water operates on this Earth. I can cloak anything if I have access to water. Ice is a very useful form of water too, don't you think?" he asked as I noticed for the first time the wavering was actually ice turning to liquid.

"You'll learn how to do it too, and much more since you control more than one element. For now, my job is to teach you to control your incredibly powerful abilities, then the teachers at the school will teach you the rest."

I nodded as he maneuvered the airship through a wall of water. The top of one of the outbuildings opened up, and we descended into the building. I'd never imagined anything like this.

I knew I didn't have much to base my perceptions on, since I'd grown up in one crappy foster home after another; but wealth on this level was mindboggling.

"Do you live here alone?" I asked.

Dr. Fagan looked at me and smiled. "Heavens no, son, this is a colony of Elementals who control water. This high up in the mountains, we are known as the ice people. But don't worry, the training facilities have been put aside for your use only while we prepare you to live at the school."

I got out of the tiny airship and followed Dr. Fagan through the door of the building and out into the mind-numbing cold. The professors kept the school grounds warm, but here, not so much. I wished I had a coat. The coat I wore in the group home in Arizona was just a thin jacket. I hadn't needed much more at school, and even over the weekend, when we'd gone down to Denver, it wasn't so cold that I needed a thick coat.

Kyle had let me borrow one of his when we were skiing. I wished I'd known where I was going; I'd have borrowed it again.

I followed the old man into another building. When we entered the main hall, he showed me a map of the community. "This is where all the houses are. You can't see them, as they're all shrouded behind the ice as mine was when we arrived, but they are here."

He looked at me then, and said, "You'll be safe here. No one in their right mind would ever attack a colony of Elementals."

The statement was meant for me. If I got out of control, I would be handled. The question probably wasn't if I would lose control, but when, and I wondered what would happen if I couldn't get it back once I'd lost it. From what Dr. Fagan had just said, I would be dispatched.

"This area is our training facility," he said, opening two large doors that led into a courtyard surrounded by ice. Even the ceiling was ice. I shivered, and Dr. Fagan laughed. "It feels cold now, but wait until we begin training. Then, you'll be thankful for the cool room."

Much of the building was made from ice. There was a skating rink on the other side of the courtyard and other smaller rooms on this side.

As we walked into the main structure, we reached more comfortable parts of the building. There was a massive fireplace in what appeared to be a sitting area with tables and chairs scattered around. The place was empty, and the fireplace was not lit. But I could tell by the well-worn furniture the room was used frequently.

Finally, we came to the other side of the large sitting area and after walking down a long hallway, entered into what I assumed was Dr. Fagan's private quarters. He showed me up the staircase to a room he said would be mine while I was here.

I was overwhelmed. How could something like this exist? I came back down after stowing my bag in the closet. Dr. Fagan was on the phone, and he turned around and winked at me. "Yes, that'll be perfect. I'll let him know," he said and hung up.

"That was your first instructor. I figured we should get the worst tests out of the way. If we can find your frustration level, we can begin working with you to control it."

"This is going to hurt, isn't it?" I asked. Dr. Fagan just smiled.

He gave me a set of exercise clothes. I could tell by how they felt they were expensive. Probably the most expensive things I'd ever worn. I had no idea how they knew my size, but I didn't spend much time thinking about it.

When I entered the courtyard, three huge men stood staring at me. There was also a little boy who looked to be about five. The strange men and the little kid in one room triggered something inside me. I would have left quickly to keep my triggers from getting the better of me, but before I could react, Dr. Fagan said, "This is your first challenge. Are you ready?"

"Ready for..."

All four men, Dr. Fagan included, lifted their hands, and a deluge of water poured from them. I didn't know what they expected me to do. Should I fight back? Should I try to get away? Finally, I decided I needed to escape. I remembered the door was behind me, so I staggered back, determined to hold my breath. I bumped into the door and felt something under my feet: the little boy.

Fuck, how did he get there? Was he breathing? I tried to feel for him, but his body was limp. No, fuck, no, I wouldn't let this happen. Not again. Not on my watch.

My mind took over automatically. Nothing was more important than protecting the child. The water kept coming, and I couldn't stop it. I didn't know how. I quickly searched the door for the knob, and finding it, I thrust it open. The boy and I were washed into the hallway. Finally, we were outside the onslaught of water.

I grabbed the child, quickly wiped the water out of my eyes, and looked to see if he was okay. The child wasn't a child at all. It was a practice dummy. I looked up straight into the eyes of Dr. Fagan.

"Interesting," he said and returned to the room. When I didn't immediately follow, he popped his head back out and asked, "Are you coming?" Like he hadn't *just* tried to drown me.

The rest of that day and every day since, they pushed me to my limits. They tried tricking me, triggering me, and forcing me to use my powers which I handled poorly at best. I'd only ever used them once.

The only times I was happy while living there were the evening phone calls I had with Lysander and sometimes with Kyle and Kaylee. Lysander was concerned about the tactics Dr. Fagan was using, but Kyle and Kaylee said they sounded pretty standard and assured me they'd been put through similar training programs when they had gone to superhero summer camps. "They're just trying to get a rise out of you to see how far you go before you break."

Finally, after a week had passed, Dr. Fagan smiled one evening after we'd finished a particularly grueling session where several men came after me with baseball bats. "You have tremendous control, Kaden. But I don't believe you understand your own powers yet. So, I will be recommending that you return here once a month for us to reevaluate you. However, as long as you maintain self-control, I have no problem recommending you remain at the school."

That night, the men who'd antagonized me all week showed up with their spouses and children. They all clapped me on the back and laughed at everything they'd put me through.

"I thought he was going to try to incinerate us that day we all tackled him and held him down," one guy said as he clapped Dr. Fagan on the back.

They were right. That had been the worst exercise of all. I wondered if they knew all the things men had done to me over the years. I'd barely maintained my self-control that day. I was screaming and crying when they let go, but I hadn't killed them. I hadn't even thought about killing them.

Getting away from them, yes, as fast as I could, but killing them, no. I knew there was a difference between these men and those who'd really wanted to hurt me. The energy in these men was easygoing, even playful. The men who'd... well, they were not these guys.

The other time I freaked out was the first test. The one where I thought the boy was in danger. I'd considered using my powers to control the situation, but Dr. Fagan had said he was testing me. The boy had to be a Water person, so despite being freaked out, my mind must've registered, even when I thought he was real, he probably wasn't in any danger.

We enjoyed a huge meal, the fire in the enormous fireplace had been built high, and the room was warm and friendly. These people were friends, and somehow, I'd begun to fit in. Once again, it was a strange sensation, as it had been when Lysander, Kyle, and Kaylee had befriended me. I considered the possibility that the world was a good place, and I'd been thrust in with the bad. Just having the ability to consider that was strange. Strange and exhilarating.

Once everyone left, I sat alone with Dr. Fagan, who was clearly three sheets to the wind. That was probably best, since I needed to confess something that might make him keep me here longer. Keep me here and away from Lysander, who I was missing more and more now that Dr. Fagan had said I was safe to be around.

"Um, I almost used my powers against you," I admitted.

Dr. Fagan turned toward me, and for the first time since I'd arrived, he didn't smile.

"Go on," he said.

"That first day I was here, when I thought the kid was drowning, I almost used my powers against you and the other guys that day."

Dr. Fagan nodded. "I felt that, and I'm glad you admitted it. But you didn't. What stopped you?" he asked.

"I remembered you saying everyone here was a Water Elemental. If the boy was an Elemental, even if he'd been real, he wouldn't have been in danger."

Dr. Fagan smiled at me and winked. "Honestly, I could've sent you back to the school that day. You proved you could rationalize when you were afraid. That's all any of us can hope for, son. We all wield significant power. Our rational brains are often all that stands between us and becoming monsters."

I thought about what he said, and it made sense. "Is that why you all live up here? So you're not worried about hurting innocent people?" I asked.

Dr. Fagan's smile faded, and he turned back toward the fire. "You're a very astute young man. I think all of us fear we'll hurt the less powerful. At least, those of us who choose to be decent people. It's easier when you can live in a world where you can't destroy others. Well...not without them doing significant damage to you in return."

We sat silently then, both of us staring into the fire.

"I asked you on the first day how long it would take you to incinerate the school and everyone in it. Do you understand now why that question was so important?"

I nodded. "I still don't know the answer. But based on when I found my powers the first time and the time it took until I had all the kids outside the building, I'd guess it was less than ten minutes. I had never used my powers before and didn't know what I was doing. Now, if I had to guess, I'd say less than a minute."

Dr. Fagan didn't respond. He just stared into the fire. "Then, for your sake and the rest of the world's, let's hope you continue to control your own mind."

Chapter Twenty-One
Lysander

I'D SPOKEN TO KADEN every night except one since he'd been gone. Yeah, I knew I was behaving like a lovesick teenager. *But I am still a teenager! So, I'm entitled.*

Kaden struck all the right chords in me. Being with him felt right somehow. More than right, it was epic.

It was Saturday morning when he returned to campus. He'd texted, telling me he was on his way back. It was a lot sooner than he'd anticipated. I was in his dorm room when he came in, and I didn't wait for him to put his bag down before I was on top of him.

He chuckled when I knocked him onto his bed. "Damn," I said as I began undressing him. "I've missed you so freaking bad!"

"Really?" he asked, surprised.

I stopped mid-button and looked at him. "Of course, we were just starting this thing, and then you disappeared for a week. You know I missed you."

"I missed you too," he said shyly.

"You okay with this?" I asked, gesturing toward the button on his shirt that I was still holding.

He smiled and nodded. "I'm more than ready, Lysander. I need you."

"Good," I said, my smile matching his. "Now get undressed."

That night as I lay in his arms, listening to him breathing. I thought of how surprised he'd been when I told him I'd missed him. That must be part of his traumatic past. I wondered if maybe I needed to learn more about what PTSD did to people. Clearly, Kaden had it, and why wouldn't he? I mean, he went through worse things than I could even imagine.

He stirred under me and whispered, "I can hear you thinking."

I chuckled. "You can't hear my thoughts. That's not one of your powers."

"No, but I can tell you're thinking hard. You do this weird thing with your nose when you're thinking about stuff."

"No I don't!" I said, and playfully slapped his chest with my hand.

"You do, and it's cute. Wanna talk about it?"

"No, well, I know you've been through a lot, and I've been raised in pretty much the best way someone can be. I wonder if maybe I'm not being supportive enough."

Kaden snorted. "You're the first person who ever cared, period. I think you're doing a lot."

I leaned up on my elbow. "Really? You're not just saying that?"

"No, I don't know much about what I feel most of the time. The past was horrible, but I don't think about it much. It's like it's shrouded or something."

I sighed. "Well, if it ever gets weird or I don't say the right thing, let me know. I really like you, Kaden, and I don't wanna fuck up just 'cause I'm ignorant."

He rolled me over on my back and climbed on top of me. "You won't fuck it up. You're perfect just the way you are."

I leaned up and kissed him. The man was truly hot as hell.

Chapter Twenty-Two
Kaden

I WAS ONLY PARTIALLY honest with Lysander. I wasn't used to people caring about me. It was good, but unnerving. When I came into my dorm room, and he all but attacked me, I was waiting for him to yell at me or be upset or break up, or something.

I wouldn't have guessed he'd missed me. Of course, I figured that out pretty quickly as he savored my body.

I had been honest about the memories of my past. I'd put those away, shelved them in a place far from my mind's reach. The man who'd pretended to be my therapist at the group home had told me that was bad, that the memories would come back to get me and cause me to explode one day, but I knew if I had those memories front and center in my mind, that was what would cause me to explode.

They were my past. Something I couldn't do anything about, so it didn't do any good fixating on them. Move forward. That was what I had to do. And after spending time with Dr. Fagan, I realized just how important it was never to be in a compromised position again. He'd told me that the first day I was there, after he and the men had all but drowned me. I was a bomb that could destroy everything in my path. Self-control was the mechanism that kept that bomb in check.

Childhood trauma, memories of the hell I went through and witnessed other kids go through, and the thought that someone could do that to me again were the biggest threats I faced when it came to self-control.

Lysander settled down on my chest and quickly fell asleep. I was still surprised at how different sex felt with him. When he touched me, my body responded in incredible ways. Not the horror I'd always associated with it.

Having him snuggled up against me made me feel protective. But deeper than that, it made me feel hopeful. That was a lot scarier than anything I'd ever experienced before. People like me didn't harbor hope. Hope made you vulnerable. A small green shoot sticking out of a concrete sidewalk for someone to stomp into smithereens. But as he lay next to me, that was the feeling I had.

For the life of me, I couldn't push that little green shoot back below the ground. I wanted what this life could be. I wanted what I could be with Lysander more than I was afraid. I knew I was being stupid, and it was probably just a matter of time before someone stomped me down, maybe even Lysander himself. But I still couldn't get myself to pull back. Now that I somewhat trusted Dr. Fagan, maybe I'd have a chat with him about what it would mean if I ever got hurt. Would that make me dangerous or someone to fear?

Chapter Twenty-Three

Lysander

Having Kaden back at school was amazing. We had a new teacher in the second-year Practicum course. Elana Efferent was a Master Elemental with the rare Fire skill combined with Air. She readily confessed to us on day one that her ability with Air was seriously limited, and she used that skill to enhance her elemental Fire skills.

The benefit was that she could let me practice absorbing her Air powers, and they didn't set me up to die. Also, Kaden could see someone with two elemental powers who integrated them effectively.

None of us were under the illusion that we mattered as much as Kaden. No, Elana had come to teach our class *for* Kaden. None of us said that to him, but since I spent a good deal of time with him outside class, I knew he'd come to the same conclusion.

Kaden was special. Dr. Aynesworth was afraid of him, but the school had to be getting some serious kudos for having a Quadripartite as a student. In our Elemental 101 class, we'd been told Kaden was the first to be discovered.

He was remarkable to watch. In Practicum, he'd begun working on each element separately. He'd used some of his Water powers while he'd been away, but Elana had him build them and use them in tedious ways.

"This goes for everyone in class," she said as Kaden was forced to move a drop of water from the front of the lab to the back and then drop it through a tiny hole in the side of a beaker. "Moving large amounts with your skill is like using gross motor skills. It's easier to run around willy-nilly than to walk a balance beam. Watch as Kaden focuses on the small drop. He has to keep the intention firmly in his mind or the drop will fall."

Kaden got to the edge of the table where the beaker sat, and the drop fell. He exhaled and collapsed into a chair next to the lab table.

"That was good, Kaden," Elana said, smiling. "Rest a bit, then try it again. The rest of you look through the notes I gave you when you came in and begin practicing using your powers' finer skills."

She came over and sat across from me. "I had to think about how to use your skills in this exercise, and to be honest, I'm not one hundred percent sure this will work. But if you can learn to siphon off small amounts of energy instead of trying to take in the other Supe's power, it could prove useful. So, your job is to practice taking only a small part of my Air power. Just a small amount, we'll begin with causing my heavy breeze to reduce to a gentle flow."

In the end, I could do it, but damn, it was the hardest thing I'd ever done. I could take all the Air energy from her, no problem, but trying to siphon it slowly or partially. That was intense.

"Damn," I said to Kaden as we sat in the student lounge, waiting for Kyle and Kaylee to finish their classes. "I'm exhausted. Thank God that's the last class of the day."

Kaden nodded, but didn't respond. "You okay?" I asked.

"Yeah, but it's strange. The more focused I am on one of my powers, the more the rest of them want to come out. It was like fighting everything in me to stay focused. Does that make sense?"

"Sort of. It's not that way for me, it's more difficult. Do you think you should mention it to Elana?"

"I did already. She said she'd discuss it with Dr. Fagan since he's officially my school advocate."

"Good, so I'm guessing they'll know how to handle it."

Kaden looked over at me and smiled. "You're always Mr. Optimistic," he teased.

"If it isn't a problem, don't turn it into one. That's a saying my mom drilled into my head when I was a kid."

"Yeah, makes sense," he said. He leaned over then and kissed me.

"Dude, all you two do is kiss," Kyle said as he came around the corner and flopped down across from us.

I laughed. "Where's your sister?"

"She got roped into doing some women's only telekinetic thing."

"And you're jealous?" I asked.

"Well, they did confirm that we're polarities. If we're stronger together, it doesn't make sense to work apart."

"Really? Dude, you're a mess. You and your sister won't be together all the time. She's got to learn how to use her powers when you aren't there. Besides, you're here at the school. You don't have to be side by side for the polarity energies to work."

He took a deep breath and sighed. "I know. It's just that we've always done things together. It's strange when we don't."

Kaden reached over and patted Kyle on the shoulder. "It'll be okay, is it harder 'cause you're twins?" he asked.

"Yeah, probably. But she's started seeing Leon too, and we spend less and less time together. It's just strange not to have her bugging the crap out of me all the time."

"So, how's it going with Terry?" I asked.

Kyle heaved a sigh. "He isn't that into me. No surprise, he's Mr. Superhero. Do you know his granddad was one of the first? No, you probably don't, and I wouldn't either, except he tells me, like, every time I come around. So, nothing is going on there."

I sat next to Kyle. "Sorry, buddy, but he's not the only Supe here. Did you notice the other day some upperclassman was checking you out?"

Kyle laughed. "You're an idiot. No one was checking me out."

We argued in good humor while he, Kaden, and I had dinner together. Afterward, we all had to get back to our studies. Professor Sturgis had piled on a ton of homework for Elemental Studies, saying we should be far enough along now to be able to pick up the pace.

Kaden and I weren't in the same class, but we had the same syllabus and professor, so we could study together. I was glad our class was too big to fit us all into one room, because having Kaden with me was distracting. Not only because he still glowed like a freaking black light bulb, but because now that black glow caused my insides to quiver in anticipation of being in bed together again.

I hadn't understood what emotions that light and his intense stare caused me to feel when I'd first met him, but I had no problem understanding them now. Kaden Pierce could melt me with his sexy eyes and aura with no effort whatsoever.

If I didn't know he was a Quadripartite, I'd argue he was an incubus or some other Supe who had the power to melt people from the inside out with their basic desire for him.

Chapter Twenty-Four

Kaden

D R. FAGAN WAS CONCERNED when I told him the more controlled I made my powers, the more they all tried to come out at once. Elana, our new teacher, and Dr. Fagan said they'd discuss it. Ultimately, they decided I should only do the concentrated experiments when I was under the supervision of the Water element people.

So, we were back to me practicing with the individual elements one at a time, which, honestly, was still pretty awesome. I could move water in an arc, and I could freeze it or turn it into steam.

I could do the same with Fire. Playing between the aspects of smoke and fire. Elana even showed me how to utilize the Air element of my abilities to cause the Fire to ignite or reduce it to a small flame deprived of oxygen.

Earth was more difficult. I ended up hanging out with three upperclassmen who were experts at using Earth energy. Of course, I was under the supervision of Elana. We moved rocks from the ground, then dissected them into different components: granite, sand, and limestone. Most of the local rocks didn't have quite as many elements to them, they were mostly granite, but I got the idea.

We also worked on the granite, using our abilities to create sculptures. The delicate work once again felt as though all my powers wanted to come out at once, so I stopped doing the sculpture aspects of the training and told Elana why.

She looked concerned and nodded, but asked me to continue with the other exercises.

Lysander and I grew closer as the months quickly passed. But during the week, we mostly stumbled home exhausted after hours spent perfecting our skills. When you watched movies with superheroes in them, none of them ever look tired after they zapped the bad guys into oblivion. But every day, Lysander and I, even the twins, would come home and crash in front of the television.

Luckily, even Professor Sturgis wasn't forcing us to read as much now. "You need to use your skills. We'll get back to reading later," he'd said when someone asked him why he was going easy on us.

Because Lysander and I had Practicum every afternoon, we were probably even more exhausted than our other freshmen. Elana didn't go easy on us just because we were still freshmen. I'm glad, in a way, that she didn't. I felt more confident about my powers, but I also understood their potential dangers. When I focused too much or fine-tuned my abilities, I could feel them trying to overtake me. That scared me more than I wanted to admit.

By the time winter break arrived, everyone was ready for some time off. One night, as Lysander snuggled into me, he asked, "Are you willing to spend Christmas with my family?"

I laughed. "Have you asked Pete if he's okay with that? Last time we were there, I thought he was going to skin me alive."

"He's all bark. Besides, now they know you saved all those kids, they think you're some sort of superhero."

I sighed. I knew he'd probably told them, but secretly I hoped my past wouldn't cause them to hate me. I'd seen the fear on the faces of everyone in my life since then, except Lysander and the twins.

Even Elana and Dr. Fagan sometimes looked afraid when they challenged me or forced me to test my powers.

"If you think they won't mind, I'd like that."

He snuggled closer, which spoke to how happy that made him. I wasn't sure how I felt. I suspected Lysander's family would be freaked out by me, and maybe that would drive a wedge between us. I kept waiting for the next shoe to drop, and I figured maybe this was it.

I reminded myself no one had ever wanted me for long. I was told when I was a baby there had been a woman I'd lived with, but that she'd died when I was still a toddler. I didn't remember her, but since then, I'd never stayed anyplace for more than a few months.

The fact that we were going on four months together unnerved me and made me itchy when I thought about it.

That small green shoot of hope was growing. In my mind's eye, it was six inches tall now. Still vulnerable, able to be taken out by anyone with half a mind to destroy it, but it was bigger than it'd ever been before.

The day before winter break, Elana pulled me aside and asked if I could come back early and spend some time working on my powers.

"Sure, um, are we going back to the Water Element community?" I asked.

"No, we're going somewhere you can let your powers flow without fear of hurting others. Unfortunately, until you let them all out, we can't know what you're capable of doing."

I looked at her, confused. "So where am I going?"

She took a deep breath. "It's an island. Mostly deserted except for a few Fire element people. The island is an active volcano. But there, you'll have all four elements at your disposal. More importantly, if you blow the island apart, no one will get hurt."

"Do you think that's a possibility?" I asked.

She chuckled nervously. "I think it's more like a probability at this point, but don't worry, the island is the perfect place to practice."

I considered that for a moment, then nodded. "When do we go?"

Elana said she'd make all the arrangements and let me know, but it would probably be the week after Christmas. Classes started back in February, and Dr. Fagan said I needed as much time as possible in case I needed to get my powers back under control once I'd unleashed them.

"That sounds scary," I said, concerned.

"You'll be safe, considering your unique blend of powers. The rest of us will be on a nearby island, far enough away that we won't be in danger, but close enough if you need us."

I nodded again but wasn't feeling confident. I was beginning to curse the powers again. They were just too much for one human to carry. I'd asked Dr. Fagan why I had all the powers when I was struggling to contain them, and he shrugged and gave me some explanation about being born with some and then probably being exposed to such extreme trauma caused the rest to develop.

That didn't answer my question. What I really wanted to know was, why me? Why the unwanted orphan that, up until the day my powers erupted, had been nothing? A nobody. Why did I have these powers I now had to learn to control?

I knew deep down I should be dead by now. People like me didn't live long. Briggs, the man who had been my handler, would've killed me now that I'd gotten too big to sell as a kid, or I'd have become like him. Knowing I would never become that kind of person, I knew I'd be dead, not going to school in a fancy superpower school in the clouds, or having Christmas dinner with an amazing boyfriend and his family.

I wasn't supposed to have friends like the twins who loved to harass me, but cared about me and my relationship with their other friend, Lysander. No, that was other people. That wasn't supposed to be me.

Chapter Twenty-Five

Lysander

"KADEN, YOU HAVE TO help. It's a family rule!"

"Honey, he's your guest. Leave him alone. Kaden, make yourself at home in the living room. We'll let you know when the meal is ready."

I gawked at my mom. "That is so not going to happen, he has two hands just like you and me, and I'm not in training to be some nineteen-fifties housewife."

"Hush your mouth," Mom said, but the slight grin didn't escape me.

Kaden was laughing in the kitchen doorway. "Libby, I truly don't mind helping. I just don't know how to cook. When it's my night to cook at school, I toss a pizza in the oven."

"That's true, he does," I admitted, "—but he can peel potatoes. Kaden, here, use this," I said as I handed him the potato peeler.

He looked at it, then at me, confused about how it worked. Mom laughed and moved me to the middle of the room as she took a potato and began showing him how to use it. "I could've shown him." I pouted.

She chuckled and ignored me. I never did have patience for teaching people stuff. She knew that, and so did I. Luckily, Kaden took to the peeling easily enough, and before long, the three of us were working in the kitchen preparing the meal.

My Aunt Teresa was in charge of bringing the meats, which for us was always ham and turkey. We were in charge of the sides. It'd been that way since my grandparents had moved into the nursing home when I was still in middle school.

Her husband, my Uncle Chuck, was a master griller and smoker, so naturally, they took on the job.

Once Kaden was done with the potatoes, Mom handed him a bowl of boiled eggs to peel and patiently showed him how. I guessed I hadn't noticed he didn't even know the basics, like peeling an egg or potato. Again, I felt like a horrible boyfriend for not knowing these things about him.

He seemed to be enjoying himself, though, so I didn't bring the party down by showing my guilt.

At three o'clock, Pete showed up, always the expert at avoiding most of the prep work. Aunt Teresa and Uncle Chuck followed shortly after carrying two big platters of smoked meats.

"So, you boys are superheroes now, huh?" Uncle Chuck asked as we were finishing our meal.

I laughed. "Not yet," I admitted.

"So, what have you learned?" Mom asked.

I thought about it for a moment. "Control mostly. When I started, I was unsure what I had or what to do with it. Now, I'm learning to use my ability to absorb other students' powers, but let the elements around me absorb them, not my body."

"That's got to be weird," Aunt Teresa chimed in.

My mother's sister was... prudish, I thought was the best word. She disapproved of powers in general. She hadn't even liked my dad because he was in the army, not a respectable job like Uncle Chuck's accounting firm. So, she almost always said something rude or inappropriate.

"Oh, I don't know that he's all that weird, Teresa. I mean, you knit, turning the hair of a sheep into doilies and stuff." Mom knew her sister well. Teresa was a well-known knitter, and her sweaters were sought after. So, she'd hit her where it mattered.

"There's a big difference between skill and... magic!" she said, turning her face up.

"Teresa, stop being an ass," Mom said, and immediately changed the subject. "So, Kaden, honey, how are you liking school?"

Kaden smiled. "It's a bit overwhelming, but I like it."

I squeezed his knee under the table, and he looked at me, his smile never leaving his face.

"So, what's your magic?" Aunt Teresa asked, and I almost choked on my last bite of roll.

"I control the four elements," he said, either not noticing or ignoring her derision.

"Control the four elements?" Uncle Chuck asked. "Like you can make it rain and stuff?"

Kaden nodded. "I can't control the weather yet, but I'm told that's something I'll be able to do eventually."

"Let's have dessert," Mom said, getting up before Aunt Teresa could say something rude. "Teresa, come help me!"

Aunt Teresa pursed her lips, but got up, putting her napkin on the table, and following Mom into the kitchen.

As soon as they were out of earshot, I whispered, "Sorry."

Kaden shrugged. Clearly, her attitude hadn't bothered him.

Uncle Chuck reached over and patted Kaden on the shoulder. "I went to school with a kid who could control water. It was cool. Actually, he used to create an above-ground pool when we were kids. You could swim into the side of it and back out. I wonder what happened to him?"

Mom and Aunt Teresa came back, and from how flushed Teresa was, I assumed Mom had laid down the law. I almost laughed since I'd been on the receiving end of that tongue-lashing many times, and I knew how it stung. I almost felt sorry for Aunt Teresa.

All talk of powers ceased, and we were back to just enjoying one another. Uncle Chuck talked about their new summer property in the mountains near Granby.

"They have the most beautiful lake up there. It's just so scenic," Aunt Teresa interrupted Uncle Chuck.

"Maybe we can come visit," Mom said, and her sister nodded. It would've been fun to give Aunt Teresa a heart attack and suggest maybe Kyle, Kaylee, Kaden, and I could visit too, but I knew better than to put fuel on a fire Mom had barely put out.

Luckily, Aunt Teresa and Uncle Chuck left earlier than usual. That meant it was just Mom, Pete, Kaden, and me.

We gathered around the coffee table in the living room, Kaden and me on the floor and Mom and Pete on the couch. We played cards like we always did on the holidays.

Kaden didn't know how to play, so we taught him *Skip-Bo* and *UNO*, which were both easy to learn. He ended up cleaning up on *Skip-Bo*.

"You're a freaking card shark," Pete said after Kaden won the third game.

"Beginner's luck," I said, and Kaden smiled. He'd been really quiet all day. I figured he must be overwhelmed by my insane family, Aunt Teresa being an ass, and Uncle Chuck clueless. But just like earlier in the kitchen, when Mom was teaching him how to cook, he seemed happy. That was all I could wish for.

I looked forward to cuddling later when I could get the full story from him. He was always quiet and reserved, but usually when we were alone, if I prodded him a little, he'd share what was on his mind.

I loved that about us, like we had something special together. Maybe it was selfish of me, but I liked being Kaden's confidant. Of course, I also enjoyed being his best friend and lover.

Chapter Twenty-Six

Kaden

C HRISTMAS WITH LYSANDER'S FAMILY was like you'd see on television. Even the snarky aunt seemed to be playing some sort of role. Mostly I watched as the family interacted. It was so utterly foreign to me that it was hard to imagine it was real.

I kept waiting for some director in the background to yell cut. When Lysander's Aunt Teresa asked me what kind of magic I did, I almost spat out the water I'd just taken a sip of. She meant it to be a slur. Of course, it didn't bother me in the least. Why would it? She was angry because someone had something she didn't. Jealousy was an emotion I understood incredibly well.

I spent most of my childhood jealous of other people. Jealous of the kids in school, when I finally got to school, for having families to go home to. Jealous of people on television who seemed to have something I never did. Jealous of kids my age that hadn't been used for sex.

Maybe I knew Aunt Teresa better than she knew herself. It was only when she was able to boast about something she had that her sister didn't that she was happy—the lake house in the mountains. I wondered if she even liked it, or whether it was just something she had that she could brag about.

"You want some more hot cocoa?" Lysander asked, pulling me from my thoughts.

"No, I'm so full. I don't know if I've ever been this full before."

Lysander chuckled. "Wait till next year when you come for Thanksgiving. That whole holiday is about stuffing yourself, then stuffing yourself again."

"What did we do tonight?" I asked, ignoring the obvious allusion to there being a next year for us.

"Tonight was about opening presents. Did you really like yours?" he asked me for the third time.

I reached over, kissed him, and showed him the pendant I was wearing. There were four stones representing the four elements. I could tell he'd spent a lot of time looking for it. I hadn't owned jewelry before, but the moment I put it on, I knew I'd never take it off.

"It's amazing, Lysander. I'm sorry I didn't get you something better."

"Shut up, seriously?" he fussed at me again.

I'd found a vein of silver running through quartz while practicing with the Earth Elementals. I didn't dare use my powers to shape it, but I asked Dennis, the de facto head of the Earth Elementals to do it for me. He was able to make a replica of Lysander's head, and the silver vein looked as if it was a crown.

It was probably hokey, but when I'd seen the rock, I'd thought of him. So, it seemed appropriate that I use that as his gift.

"I'm King Lysander!" he'd said when he opened the present.

His mom snickered and said, "More like queen," causing us all to laugh, except Lysander, who gave his mom a look... until he too cracked up.

"I'd have bought you something nice, but I still don't have money."

"You created me a one-of-a-kind piece of art, Kaden. That's the best gift you could give me. Not only is it beautiful, but I can't believe you got it to look so much like me."

"I didn't," I said, shrugging. "Dennis did, but maybe after the next lesson, I'll be able to use my power to make more refined things."

Lysander looked sad. "I wish you didn't have to go."

I sat silently staring at the wall as Lysander leaned against my side.

"I have to. I have to figure out what my powers can and can't do. More importantly, I have to figure out if I can control them."

He looked me in the eye. "Are you concerned about that?" he asked.

I sighed. "Yeah, Lysander, I'm concerned about it a lot. I haven't been able to push my powers to the limits for fear of hurting... well, you mostly, but the other students too."

He lay back down and rubbed my arm. "It'll be okay. I trust Elana. She's not like Dr. Bisbee, she actually cares about us."

I nodded, knowing he couldn't see me. "Dr. Fagan will be there too, along with some other experts and specialists. At least, that's what she told me. The best part is that if I blow the island away, no one is close enough to get hurt."

"You think you're gonna blow an island up?"

"No idea. To me, these powers don't feel as big as everyone makes them out to be. They're just there. But I know what I did. I know what can happen when I don't have control, or don't know what I'm doing. I just..."

"You're a hero, Kaden. You saved a bunch of kids from horrors only you and they understand. You're gonna eventually have to believe that and stop seeing yourself as someone who did wrong."

We'd had the same conversation multiple times, but I still saw myself as the monster. I'd killed the bad guys, but I didn't know what was happening. Luckily, the kids didn't get caught up in the chaos that day. No matter what Lysander said, that day I *was* a monster. If I let myself lose control, I could and would be again. That was why I had to go to the island with Elana and Dr. Fagan. That was why I had to push myself to the limit.

Monday morning came, and I got up feeling more than a little trepidation. Lysander had held me tightly all night, even as he slept. I hadn't slept at all. Mostly I stared at the ceiling in his room.

It wasn't as simple as Elana said. I knew I could kill myself. I ultimately accepted it as inevitable if I was being honest.

We hadn't had sex since we'd gotten to Lysander's home since it was his mom's house. But we'd cuddled every night. Last night having him hold me as I processed the concern and fear of facing what could be my doom felt right too. Like I was a soldier going off to war.

Dr. Fagan's airship landed on the street outside the house. I stuffed my bag full of my clothes, and Lysander agreed to take my presents, which included everything from clothes to a deck of *Skip-Bo* and *Uno* cards, with him back to the school.

I hugged him one last time, then thanked his mom and Pete for letting me stay over the holiday.

The next moment, Dr. Fagan was speeding into the sky and toward... well, honestly, I had no idea where we were headed. Of course, with the G-force pushing my body back against the seat, I didn't have much chance to ask him.

We whirled through the air and landed outside the school, where a larger airship awaited us. When Dr. Fagan looked over, he asked, "What? You thought we'd be going all the way to the South Pacific in this?" He got out laughing.

I had to slowly take a couple of breaths before exiting the vehicle. The first time I'd ridden with Dr. Fagan, I thought he was trying to test me. Now that I'd ridden with him a few times, I understood he was just insane. Or maybe I was the insane one for getting into his airship.

The larger vessel was luxurious, to say the least. You could sit in a window seat, or if you were afraid of heights, you could sit inside and away from the windows. I didn't think I was afraid of heights. If I was, Dr. Fagan's driving would've cured me by now, so I sat right next to the huge windows looking out over the landscape.

As we flew, I helped myself to drinks and snacks. I could have watched a movie, but I had a cup of hot cocoa, which I now associated with Lysander. Slowly sipping it as I watched the incredible landscape unfold below me was soothing.

The trip wasn't a fast one, even in the airship. Flying twice as fast as modern jets, it still took eight hours. I hadn't slept the night before, so I dozed a lot, which surprised me. I didn't tend to sleep when I was nervous. There were times when I'd been locked away in the rooms under Briggs's supervision that I hadn't slept for days, maybe a week.

I woke up just as we arrived. I guess part of me was at peace because even if I died doing this, I would've at least gone out through my own actions, and not because I was being forced to, or because I was someone's victim.

The island was... well, there wasn't much to see. I'd heard of volcanic islands like Hawaii, so I'd envisioned a beautiful tropical rainforest paradise. This was definitely not paradise. It was desolate, and the air smelled like sulfur. "Um, what is this?" I asked Elana.

"Hector Island. It's only fifteen years old, rose out of the sea in less than twenty minutes," she said. "How do you feel, Kaden?"

I checked myself and shrugged. "Okay."

She shook her head. "You should feel energized being this close to a young active volcano. It's the very essence of your Fire Elemental abilities."

I closed my eyes and focused again, but I felt nothing.

When I opened my eyes and shrugged, she looked disappointed. "I don't quite understand your skills, Kaden, but that's okay. It doesn't impact what we're going to do here," she said.

A couple of small wooden huts sat on the island's edge, almost touching the sea, and I was shown into one of the rooms. "You'll be staying here," Elana announced. "The rest of us will stay about fifty miles away at Crater Island. You can communicate with us through your microphone, as long as you don't destroy it. If you do, we have a satellite system dedicated to this project, and a drone will be sent out to communicate with you."

I nodded, and she put her hands on my shoulders. "Okay, chin up, we're going to fly over to the other island, and when we land, you can start your experiments."

I went into the hut and began exploring shortly after the rest of the crew left. I hadn't gotten to know any of the specialists or experts as they'd called them. One man I met named Sofie had ridden on the airship with us, but no one took the time to explain what he did. I hadn't asked. I figured if I needed to know, someone would tell me.

"Kaden, do you copy?" Elana's voice came through the speaker.

"Yeah, I'm here."

"Good, okay, we've safely landed. Are you ready to begin?"

"Sure, I guess," I said with trepidation.

"Okay, good. Go to the second hut, not the one you're sleeping in, but the one next to it." I hadn't explored that building yet, so I was curious about what they'd put out for me. When I walked in, I was shocked to see a massive boulder in the middle of the room. "Okay, I'm here."

"Good. Your first experiment is to identify the individual grains of sand in the boulder. I want you to focus on those grains of sand. When you can feel them, let me know, and I'll tell you what to do next."

I took a deep breath and focused on the boulder. There were several elements within the rock, but sand was the least prevalent. *Most of the stuff we think of as sand is silica*, I said to myself as I searched the rock for that element. "Okay," I think I've found it all."

"Good, very good," Elana said through the speaker. "Now, I want you to remove the grains of sand one at a time and place them in the bowl sitting on the table next to the front door. Do that until you've removed all of them from the boulder."

I concentrated and found one of the grains of sand closest to the outside of the rock and, with my powers, released it. I moved it quickly to the bowl, then did the same thing again.

Usually, with this kind of concentration, my powers would try to force their way out of my body. But not here. It only took me a few minutes to remove all the sand particles from the boulder. "I'm done," I said.

"Did you need to resist your powers?" Dr. Fagan asked. I could tell he was disappointed.

"No, they didn't surge like they usually do."

"Interesting," I heard Elana say in the background. They didn't switch off the microphone, and I could hear a group of people discussing what the problem could be. Finally, Dr. Fagan came back on.

"Kaden, let's experiment with the water next. Do you remember the experiment you did in the classroom where you moved a drop of water from one part of the room to the next?"

"Yes," I said.

"I want you to do that again, but this time if your powers try to surge, don't hold them back, okay?"

"Okay," I agreed and looked around, finding a beaker just like the one in the classroom on a shelf. I found a small bottle of water in the opposite corner of the room, opened it, and with my powers, gently lifted a drop of water into the air and moved it slowly to the beaker.

"Um, I did it," I announced to the room.

"No surge?" Dr. Fagan asked.

"No, nothing."

We did several more experiments, then the whole crew came back to the island and had me repeat them—still nothing. The surge didn't happen to me here.

"Could it have something to do with the school?" the man named Sofie asked.

"No, that's unlikely. Kaden, you can come back to the main island with us. There's no need for you to stay here when your powers aren't pressing you," Dr. Fagan said, and we all boarded the airship and flew back to the main island.

It looked more like what I'd expected. The island was covered in tropical rainforest. Coconut palms swayed in the wind, and bird and insect noises surrounded me. "Um..." I said as I left the ship, "...this is an improvement in accommodations."

Elana came down the stairs behind me, chuckling. "Yeah, but you don't get to blow this island up."

I smiled and saluted her. "Got it, no blowing up this pretty tropical island."

Over dinner, we sat around and discussed the circumstances. There were ten people present. I'd been introduced to them, but I had no idea which powers each possessed. I wished I had the Terrestrial power of discernment. We had a senior at school who had that ability, and she could identify everyone with powers, except mine. She kept saying mine were all muddled up, which was annoying, and she was all too happy to say that over and over, so I mostly avoided her.

"If it's not isolation, it has to be the elevation of the school," one of the women said.

"Kaden, when we went up in the airship, did you feel a surge in power?" Elana asked.

"No, I've only felt the surge at school."

Dr. Fagan concentrated on me. "Was it only in your Practicum class that you felt it?" he asked.

"Mostly. But no," I said, "I felt it before. Once was the first time I felt my powers, the second time was when I saw Lysander for the first time."

Dr. Fagan chuckled. "And when was the next time you felt it?" he asked.

I thought for a moment and remembered the day the twins had knocked the snow down onto the soccer team. "When I saw Lysander again."

Dr. Fagan shook his head, and I noticed several others had picked up on the same thought. "Lysander is your polarity." He looked at the group and shrugged. "I can't believe we missed it. Kaden is already powerful, probably the most powerful being on the planet. When he's with his polarity, those powers are magnified. No wonder he feels like they're about to burst out of him."

Several people in the room nodded this time.

"So," Elana asked, "—we need to get Lysander here?"

Dr. Fagan looked at her, then over at me. "Lysander might be at risk if you let your powers go when he's in your presence. Did you feel the same surge of power when you were at my cabin?"

"Yeah, not as strong, but it was definitely there."

"So, that's fifty, maybe sixty miles from the school. It might work to have Lysander here on the island. We could even use Orag Island, which is fifteen miles closer if necessary."

The table erupted in discussion, with several people arguing that Orag was too close to the blast radius and that we needed to keep a full fifty miles from the blast site to remain safe.

Someone else was arguing that it was unethical to put Lysander at risk. They needn't have worried. I'd die myself before I did anything to put Lysander in danger.

Finally, after thirty minutes of arguing, Dr. Fagan stood up. "It's the only way. If the boy will come, we have to try."

"Sir, I won't do anything to put Lysander at risk. I-I'm sorry, but I won't," I said and stood up. "I know I'm a danger, and people fear me, but I won't intentionally hurt anyone." I almost qualified that with the men I'd killed, but decided to avoid that conversation. "The one person who means the most to me in life is Lysander

Phillips. I'd rather stay away from him for the rest of my life than put him in danger."

The group looked at one another and then back at me. An older woman said, "That's an option. We've used forced separation of polarities to penalize Supes who've abused their powers. But, son, it's soul-crushing to live without your polarity once you've found them."

"Not only that, you and your polarity are boyfriends," Elana said. "That makes it even harder."

"I'll do it if it means he'll be safe. Wait, how did you know?"

She smiled and winked. "We all know, honey," she said.

Dr. Fagan shook his head. "It doesn't mean he'll be safe. Or anyone on the planet will be safe."

He looked at me for a long time before he sighed. "Son, do you remember when we first met, I told you how important it is for you to have people in your life?"

I nodded, remembering our first strange meeting. "Good, because the one thing we know about Supes is the ones who are isolated are almost always the ones to pose a threat to the planet. Not just humans but the actual planet itself."

He turned toward the window and looked out over the ocean. "We can't afford for you to isolate yourself. Even if you were totally healthy, raised in a stable, loving family, you'd still be susceptible to bad things if you isolated yourself." He turned back toward me then and made eye contact. "When you consider you are the most powerful Supe we've encountered in all our time studying Supes, and your history is littered with abuse, it's beyond imperative for you to keep healthy connections between you and other human beings. Otherwise, you could be the very end of life on this planet."

Surely he was exaggerating. I accepted my powers were big, but they made it sound like I was an apocalyptic bomb. I looked around the room to see if maybe someone's expression would contradict what Dr, Fagan had said. None did.

"Why can't you remove my powers?" I asked, suddenly afraid.

"It's physically impossible. You are too powerful."

"Wait," I said, moving away from the group and backing up toward the door. "You're telling me, my relationship with Lysander and the twins is the only thing keeping me from blowing the world to pieces?"

Dr. Fagan shrugged. "Possibly, we don't know. In fact, we can't know. What we do know is that you are different from anyone or anything we've seen before. We can contain that energy to some degree, but only to the degree you allow us to contain you."

"I don't understand. Why haven't you told me this before?"

"You weren't ready," Dr. Fagan said to the silent room.

"And I'm ready now?" I asked, panicking.

"No, you probably aren't, but you do need to understand the stakes, Kaden. Lysander, like it or not, plays a very significant role in your emotional equilibrium, not to mention your powers. You can't dismiss and avoid him for the rest of your life." Dr. Fagan looked over at the older woman who'd suggested it, and she blushed.

"I need some time to think. This is just too much."

No one tried to stop me as I dashed out of the small hut and darted into the forest.

I found a small stream that flowed down a steep incline, and I assumed out into the ocean. I hadn't cried in years—more years than I could remember—but the tears came unbidden now. I lay in a small clearing next to the little stream and cried for what felt like hours.

I really was a monster. I was the doomsday creature one of my foster moms used to read us from the last book in the Bible. I was the seven-headed, whatever it was. Did I even have the power not to be a monster?

I heard a noise, and somehow, I knew it was Dr. Fagan coming to find me.

He sat on a rock not far from where I lay. He didn't say anything for a long time, just let me lie there and cry. "Son, I know this is difficult, but you have a right to know who and what you are. You also have a right, and maybe even a responsibility, to understand how important it is to control what you have, to keep everyone around you safe."

I nodded. I wasn't angry at him for telling me, I was angry at myself for being this way.

"I'm gonna tell you my story, it's not as difficult as your life, but it holds some similarities."

Dr. Fagan told me about when he was young, how he'd grown up in a very religious home. They believed special powers were evil and came from the devil. So, they kicked him out when he got angry with his sister and caused the plumbing to explode.

"I hated myself for having powers, Kaden, and as a result, I isolated myself from the world, living in an old cabin on the property I now own and live on with my friends and family."

I sat up, intrigued by where his story was going. "Did you do something? Is that why you're so against isolation?" I asked.

He nodded. "It's not something I like to talk about. I ended up getting angry when a man trespassed on my property. He was being a jerk, but what I did, well, he didn't deserve what happened to him."

"So, you did the same as I did, to the men in the trafficking house?"

He nodded. "I understand what it feels like to be a pariah. I understand how you blame yourself and how easy it is to force yourself into a small space to try to be small and disappear. But I'll tell you now, that way leads to disaster."

"Tell me how the community grew to what it is now."

Dr. Fagan chuckled. "Well, I met Erudo. I knew about the school, but hadn't paid much attention to its existence. I was arrested after the incident, and Erudo bailed me out of jail. He got the charges dropped, and he took me under his wing. He helped me overcome my hardships and became a de facto dad to me." Dr. Fagan looked sad. "He remained that until he died."

"You created the community after he died?" I asked.

"No, sorry, son, I digress. There were so many people like me back then—people who'd acquired powers either by being born with them or the ones who'd woken up one day with them. There didn't seem to be any pattern to who acquired them and who didn't." He paused for a moment, and I knew he was thinking about all the theories. We'd discussed these in our orientation classes. One theory was that we'd become supers because of genetic traits. Others thought it was due to exposure to radiation, or other such chemicals that caused trauma to the human DNA... no one knew for sure.

"So, with Erudo's assistance—" Dr. Fagan continued, "—we began creating guild-like organizations. I went back to the old cabin, bought the land from the government, and built the Water Elementals' winter clan. I continued studying at the school until I got my PhD., but we built that community over time into what it is today."

He looked at me, smiling. "We used to call ourselves the mountain of misfits."

I was getting it, seeing his point finally. "You think I should let Lysander be a part of this experiment."

"It doesn't really matter what I think, Kaden. What do you think?"

"I just wanna protect him," I said, and the tears started falling again.

"Then protect him. Kaden, you're the most powerful Supe on the planet. I don't think a person can be safer than under your protection."

I snort-chuckled at that. "I don't know what the hell I'm doing. How can I protect him?"

Dr. Fagan came over and mussed my hair, like I was a little kid, and said, "You just do it. Now, come on back. The group are worried we overdid it, and I'm starving. The locals have put on a pig roast for us, and it'll be done soon. We don't want to offend our hosts now, do we?" he asked, and handed me a pack of tissues from his pocket.

I took out several and attempted to clean myself up. "No, we don't want to offend the locals. I'll call Lysander first, though. I want him to know what we're asking of him. And, Dr. Fagan, if he says no, everyone has to be okay with it, okay?"

"Of course, Kaden. No one should force anyone to put their lives in danger. That needs to be each individual's choice."

When I finally called Lysander, I told him everything that had happened that day. I told him I was basically a doomsday bomb that could go off at any moment, then waited for him to tell me to get lost. When he told me he cared about me, and that if I wanted to blow the world up, that wouldn't stop his feelings, I laughed. "You're a freaking nut."

"Yeah, but you like me."

"I do like you, Lysander. I like you maybe too much."

"Nah, it can never be too much," he said.

"So, they want me to ask you to come out and join us at the experiment site. But before you say yes, it's dangerous, Lysander. You're my polarity. We've pretty much proven that now, so if you're around me, my powers are immense and, well, they even think I might blow up an island."

"Okay, when do I come? We can blow it up together, if that's what it takes."

"Wait, you should think about it, Lysander. It's really dangerous, and I don't know if I can keep you safe."

'I'll keep myself safe, Kaden, and it's no more dangerous for me than it is for you. Of course, I wanna come. Hell, I wanted to go with you every time you left to work on your stuff. You forget you're my polarity too. I feel as empty as you do when you leave."

I sighed deeply. "Okay, I'll let them know. Then, when you get here, we'll work out how best to keep you safe. But if we can't come up with a plan we're both comfortable with, I'm not willing to risk it, okay?"

He chuckled. "Okay, but meanwhile, tell me they have a private room we can share where no one will bother us, 'cause it's been way-too damned long since, well, you know!"

"Do you only think about sex?" I asked, teasing.

"When it comes to you, yes!"

"I miss you, Lysander. I know I'm selfish, but I can't wait to see you."

"It's not selfish. It's awesome," he said, comforting me.

"Kaden, supper's ready!" Elana called from outside the hut.

"If she's outside, and I heard that, then you need to tell them we need a more private room," Lysander said, and I almost choked.

"I should probably go. See you soon?"

"See you soon," he replied, laughing.

The rest of the night was amazing. The locals had done an enormous pig roast and danced the evening away in front of fires on the beach. Just knowing Lysander was coming was enough to make my world significantly happier. I hadn't even known I was depressed until then. I guessed I was more hooked on him than I ever imagined. Lysander was more than my polarity. He was my source of happiness. He was my hope.

Chapter Twenty-Seven
Lysander

T HE MORNING AFTER MY discussion with Kaden, an airship was waiting for me in front of my mom's house. "Now, where are you going again?" Mom asked.

"I'm not exactly sure, but somewhere in the South Pacific."

"I don't like this, Lysander. You're going somewhere blind, and didn't Kaden say it could be dangerous?"

I kissed her cheek. "Mom, this is what I signed up for. It's part of the gig. I'll be fine because Kaden will be there. Trust me."

"I don't trust *them*," she said. I knew by them she meant other Supes. Since Lowen, the first-known superhero found her powers in the early sixties, the world had developed a love-hate relationship with Supes.

Mom had tried to discourage me from the moment she got the call from my high school principal saying I'd developed *some kind of power* to fend off Jeff Jones. I probably should've taken her advice, but something compelled me forward. Now I had Kaden and two of the best friends I'd ever had in the twins, I knew I'd made the right decision.

"Mom, I *am* one of them." She sighed at that and kissed my cheek. "I'll call and let you know what's going on as soon as I know. But don't freak out if I don't call you for a day or two."

She grabbed my coat and stopped me in my tracks. "That's bull, and you know it. I think I'm doing pretty good, considering you're only eighteen." She sighed, and I could see the internal war she was having between wanting to protect me and needing to let me be my own person. "The least you can do is call me the moment you land and let me know where you are."

I wasn't able to smother my smile. Libby Phillips would always be my mom, even if the world turned upside down and I became a superhero.

"Love you, Mom," I said as I dashed out the door and into the airship.

I was vibrating with excitement about the adventure. Kaden had told me about the things he'd been doing when he went to work with Dr. Fagan and the Water Elementals. I knew I wouldn't be much help, but at least I could watch and see what he was learning.

When we finally landed, I launched myself into Kaden's waiting arms and was pleased when he embraced me and swung me in a circle. "God, I can't believe you talked them into letting me come," I said excitedly.

Dr. Fagan came up behind us and said, "Well, it was actually *us* talking *him* into letting you come."

Kaden looked down. "This is dangerous, Lysander. I didn't want to put you in danger's path."

I kissed his adorable mouth and smiled. "I can't think of any place I'd rather be. Besides, you said the island was ugly and smelled like sulfur. This looks like paradise."

Kaden chuckled. "This isn't the island I'm working on."

"Oh, that makes sense," I quickly said. "Show me around."

"We should probably get to work," Dr. Fagan said, but when we ignored him, he just chuckled. "Okay, you have some time. Kaden, be at the main hut in one hour!"

Kaden showed me around the small island. At one time there had been a volcanic cone in the center, but that had long ago eroded and was now covered in lush forest. The smell of tropical flowers was intoxicating and occasionally hit us in the face as we walked through the thick jungle.

When we came to a small stream, Kaden sat down and motioned for me to sit next to him.

"You look concerned," I said, becoming worried myself.

"I am, Lysander. This isn't a vacation, it's serious and dangerous. When I was working on the island by myself, I didn't feel out of control at all. Now you're here, I can feel my powers buzzing inside me. As my polarity, you magnify what I have, and that's sorta scary."

"Why does it scare you?" I asked, confused.

"I'm not sure I can control it when you're around," he admitted.

"What? So you're breaking up with me?" I asked, suddenly feeling alarmed.

"No, that would break *me*. I'm just telling you why I'm concerned about you being here."

I nodded. "So, you're here to learn your limits, right? If my being here helps with that, that's a good thing. Not something to be worried about."

He looked at me for several long moments before he sighed. "I just want you to be safe."

I smiled at him, taking his face between my hands. I wondered if he knew how gaga I was over him. "I'll be fine. I doubt they'd let the islanders stay here if you were a danger to them. And Dr. Fagan and Elana are here, so they must think it's safe."

"Maybe," he said, then kissed me before he lay back on the soft grass.

I lay down next to him, enjoying his smell and the warmth of his body next to mine.

"So, what do they plan for you to do?" I asked.

"It's pretty spur-of-the-moment stuff. They want me to focus my energy on small tasks, then when the pressure builds, they want me to let it go and see what happens."

"That's what scares you?" I could feel him nodding. "I'll be here, Kaden, if you need me. I'll be right here."

Chapter Twenty-Eight

Kaden

LYSANDER STAYED ON CRATER Island as I was flown back to the volcanic one. Once the airship was safely out of range, I was told to begin the experiments again. But it was a bust. Lysander was too far away. So, they all regrouped on the smaller Orag Island, on the opposite side of this island from Crater.

This time when I began the experiment, I immediately felt Lysander's pull. Although not as powerful as the feeling of losing control was in school, when he was right next to me, the surge still hit me hard.

I'd worked so hard for so long to hold in that surge, it was virtually impossible for me to let go. Finally, after sweating bullets for five minutes trying to let go but unable to, I gave up.

"I'm sorry, I'm just too afraid I'll hurt someone."

Elana and Dr. Fagan tried to talk me down, and I tried again after each of their pep talks, but the fear was still too great.

"Kaden, listen to me," Lysander said, and just hearing his voice helped soothe me and calm the fear building inside me. "You need to try again, but this time I'll stay on the intercom with you. Okay?"

"Okay," I said, feeling very small suddenly.

"So, focus on the task, then when you feel the surge coming, go ahead and let me know."

I did as he asked. This time when the surge began to press against me, I panicked. "Okay!" I said nervously.

"Listen to me, baby. It's okay. You can let the power come out. You're far enough away from us that we'll be safe. Just let it go."

As Lysander soothed me, I released my control on the surge. The power began to seep out, slowly at first, but the more I opened, the faster it flowed, reminding me of a volcano, not unlike the one I was standing on.

The power erupted out of me, and I naturally leaned back and let it flow up and out of my mouth and hands. I couldn't scream. The power was overtaking me. My body was literally disintegrating around me. It was too much, I was destroying myself, but now that the pressure was being released, nothing I could do would stop it.

Tears streaked down my face as I realized I couldn't hear Lysander's voice. I must've destroyed the radio. I knew that would be the last time I heard his voice. I'd never see him again.

As the power overtook me, and my body disappeared around the intensity of the powers coming out of me, my mind ceased to worry. I became the very powers I'd held so tightly inside. I was no longer me. I was the elements *around* me. I was life and death, creation and destruction. I was the universe itself.

Chapter Twenty-Nine

Lysander

WE WATCHED AS A pulsar of light shot up from Hector Island. The radio went dead just before we saw the beam, and I knew Kaden's power had been released. Within seconds of seeing the pulsar, a sound wave hit us, knocking us all to the ground.

The noise rendered us all deaf, and a strange loud sound echoed in my head. I struggled to my feet just in time to see Hector Island burst apart and disappear below the waves. "Kaden!" I screamed although I couldn't hear my voice.

"Kaden!" I yelled again and again! "No, no, I can't lose you!" I cried and fell to my knees on the beach facing where the island once stood. Someone put their arms around me. Then quickly, they were removed, and I looked up just in time to see a wave at least twenty feet high barreling toward us.

I turned to see Dr. Fagan and two other men working to control the wave, but it was too much for them. We were all going to drown. Nevertheless, part of me didn't mind. If Kaden was gone because I'd encouraged him to let go and destroy himself, I didn't deserve to live. I deserved to go out the same way he had.

"Forgive me, Kaden," I said, and closed my eyes before the wave overtook me.

Nothing happened. The wave should've hit us, but when I opened my eyes, it was gone. I looked around and saw the shock on everyone's faces. They were just as surprised as I was that the tsunami hadn't washed us away.

Seconds later, we felt rather than heard another sound wave. This one was followed by an explosion that burst from the sea where Hector Island once stood. The volcano was erupting again. If it wasn't bad enough that the explosion had swept Kaden away, now his fate was truly sealed by a subsequent eruption just like the one that had created the island.

It only took moments to realize something was wrong. It wasn't a natural phenomenon. The island was growing too quickly. It was already twice the size it had been before it exploded. Fire and ash bellowed into the air, making it impossible to see.

My hearing had still not improved, but I felt someone's hand on my shoulder. Dr. Fagan was behind me and pushing me toward one of the huts that sat back from the beach. The island was more a knoll than an island, with sand all around it and a small forest in the middle. The huts sat next to the forest.

At first, I didn't know why they wanted me to move, but when I turned back, I saw a distinct ash cloud coming toward us. So, if we weren't going to be killed by the wave, the pyroclastic flow would get us. The huts wouldn't keep us from dying. I'd watched too many shows about Pompei to know that. I shook my head. No, I would stay here and take whatever was coming. I'd rather be out in the open anyway.

This time I didn't close my eyes as the cloud reached the shore. I would die facing it. But just as the cloud reached us, it turned to dust and fell into the ocean. Still, a hot blast of air hit me, but it wasn't dangerous, just a remnant of what had been there.

It was the first time I'd considered that what was happening was being controlled by Kaden. I looked up at the sky, where ash and fire burst into the stratosphere. The island was growing at incredible speed.

One thing was clear. It wouldn't take long for the island's growth to reach us here.

I sat down and watched. The rest of the crew was hidden inside the huts behind me. If I hadn't known Kaden was behind it, if he wasn't the embodiment of it, I'd have been afraid too. But now I knew, I was no longer afraid.

Within minutes, the island grew large enough that it was less than a mile from where I sat. Hot lava rolled down the sides, and I could smell the brimstone as it came closer. In anyone's mind, this would be the part that destroyed us. But if the tidal wave hadn't gotten us, if the pyroclastic cloud hadn't gotten us, the burning mass of earth wouldn't either.

Sure enough, just as the island got close enough that I could feel its heat, it began to grow around the knoll. The cliffs towering above us were hundreds of feet high. As the island surrounded us, the heat became almost too intense. I scampered back, shielding my face. The forests began to catch fire, and I knew it was just a matter of time before we succumbed to the heat as well.

Just then, a whirlwind, like a tornado, swept in around us, the air significantly cooler, and even though the huts disintegrated around the crew hiding in them, no one was hurt. We were lifted higher and higher until we were above the growing land mass.

I didn't try to crouch as the others had. Instead, I stood and watched, determined to see whatever I could. As the whirlwind touched the ocean, we were immediately surrounded by water instead of smoke and debris.

Momentarily, as the smoke cleared and was replaced with water, I saw the smoke, ash, and steam and knew it was looking at me. I knew it was Kaden, and I smiled and threw him a kiss just as the water replaced the smoke.

I knew immediately where we were going. Kaden was sending us back to Crater Island. It only took a few minutes for us to arrive, and the whirlwind set us gently on the sandy beach. We were all soaked, covered in smoke and sand, and I didn't think any of us had regained our hearing yet. But none of us were seriously harmed.

The island residents rushed toward us and helped us off the beach, checking for injuries. I knew there wouldn't be any, since my boyfriend was entirely in control.

My boyfriend. I watched as the monstrous burning mass of land continued to grow. How could that be *my* boyfriend? I laughed and knew it didn't matter how powerful Kaden was, he was just that, he was mine. I knew I loved him with everything that was in me. I knew at that moment that I would always love Kaden Pierce. And since he was literally creating an island, I didn't worry about whether I'd known him long enough or not. Conventions didn't seem to apply to us any longer.

Chapter Thirty

Kaden

ALL FOUR ELEMENTS WERE testing me, challenging me. It was as if they dared me to relax my grip on them. All four elements, one after another, went after my loved one. The first one, the tsunami, scared me. I almost lost a grip on the powers surging through me.

Something deep inside me knew if I wavered, it would spell doom and disaster for Lysander and the men and women with him.

So, I forced the sea to flatten, and it did, almost gleefully. Then the cloud of ash and fire lunged for them. Just as with the sea, I forced it to stand down, and it did. The island wanted to form. I knew what I was doing was allowing it to do what it would do naturally, given a million years or so.

Through me, the Earth was building itself, growing and expanding. It was wild and out of control. Scarier in some ways than the other elements had been. As the wall of burning earth expanded toward the small knoll where

Lysander stood, I forced it to surround them instead of destroying it. It fought me harder than the Air element in the form of the pyroclastic flow. The Earth wanted destruction. It was thriving on the chaos. But it had no choice but to surrender to my will when I forced it.

I knew Fire was coming. The cloud of superheated ash could've been the Fire element, but I knew it was only there as a tag along with Air. So, when the small knoll, now completely surrounded, began to burn, I used Air to lift Lysander and the crew out of the deepening hole they were in.

Air obeyed me with no hesitation this time. It was like a horse that'd been broken and enjoyed running with its owner on its back.

The moment the whirlwind I created opened up, Lysander was there, standing, facing me. He even threw me a kiss. He knew. He could tell who and what I was, and he still threw me a kiss. That realization echoed through me, and all that was in me vibrated with happiness.

When he was safely released on Crater Island, I focused on the task at hand. I'd established my role with each of the four elements, not in a controlling way, but with very clear boundaries. They were happy to have me. They were just part of me, and there was a promise that they would be from now on.

The island grew and grew until it had eaten up five smaller islands, not unlike the knoll Lysander had been on. This time, there was no forcing the earth around the islands. They were simply absorbed into the growth.

We, the four elements and I, worked together all day and the night and the following day before I could finally tell the earth was tiring and the growth of this now colossal island would soon end.

By nightfall, I could feel the volcanic forces under the island begin to core up and seal. I knew once it was done, there would be no volcanic activity on this island ever again. But knowing that, I could still sense where the next island would begin to form. But not for many centuries, maybe millennia from now.

As the elements began to return to their restful state, I turned back toward Crater Island and began moving my physical form in that direction.

As I got closer, the sun slowly setting behind me, I felt my molecules coming back together into their familiar places. By the time I reached the shore, I was back in my human form. Even though I was unclothed and had yet to grow back my hair and nails, I was human once again when my feet touched the beach.

Lysander immediately rushed for me, but was held back by Elana and Dr. Fagan.

"Let me go!" he demanded, and when they did, he rushed into my arms. "Oh my God, Kaden, that was magnificent," he said, when he landed in my embrace.

"I think you may be the only person who thinks so," I said as I looked into the concerned faces of the men and women standing on the shore.

Lysander pulled back, tears in his eyes, and smiled. "They don't understand. I do. I felt you. I was there as you expanded and grew. I don't... I can't explain it, but I-I understand," he said as he hugged me tightly.

Tears were in my eyes now too. "I love you, Lysander."

He nodded against my chest. "Yeah, I love you too, and a whole lot more than that, but I don't have words for it."

I kissed his forehead. "Yeah, that's how I feel too. Shall we go deal with the troops?" I asked.

"You might want to put some clothes on. I mean, I don't mind the view, but I don't really wanna share that part of you."

"Yeah, I agree. I'll get dressed. You tell them I'll be right back."

I rushed past the freaked-out crew into the hut where my clothes were and quickly got dressed. I looked at my nails, and they still hadn't grown back. When I looked in the mirror I was shocked to see what I looked like with no hair. "Damn, I hope this isn't a permanent situation," I said, concerned because I looked pretty creepy with no hair or eyebrows.

When I came out, there was a loud cheer from the beach to my left. I looked over to see the villagers had built huge fires and were all chanting, "Gedi, Gedi, Gedi."

Confused, I walked toward the group of still freaked-out team members.

Lysander quickly came over and stood next to me, forcing me to put my arm around his shoulder. "So, that happened," I said, hoping for levity.

No one moved. Lysander looked at me, and said, "Too soon, honey."

I laughed. "Okay, stop being so freaked out. You wanted me to come and get control of my powers. That's what's happened."

"You built an island," Elana said. "A really big island."

"Well, not exactly. The elements built the island. They wanted to, and they were going to do it anyway. I just allowed them to do it faster."

Dr. Fagan shook his head. "What do you mean *they* wanted to?"

I took a deep breath. "While I was helping the elements build the island, I was the elements. I still had my own personality, I wasn't completely dissolved, but I wasn't just myself either. I was... them. Does that make sense?" I asked, hoping they would understand.

They all shook their heads. "Son, we're all elementals here. Each of us has a unique skill or ability with the four elements, but no, none of us commune with them. They are not corporeal or sentient beings to us."

I took another deep breath, knowing I couldn't share my thoughts and communicate what I'd experienced.

"Kaden is different from the rest of you and the rest of humanity, I guess. He isn't just an elemental who can control the different elements. He is them. Kaden is the Earth, the universe itself," Lysander said.

I looked at him strangely. He'd described it perfectly in a way I knew I never could. I didn't have the words or the ability to communicate that well.

"How did you know?" I asked.

Lysander chuckled. "I told you I was there with you. Not at first, I was afraid. The water, then the pyroclastic cloud, then when I saw you'd forced them both to leave us alone, I knew it was you. You were the elements building the island. Once that realization hit me, I was with you. Like I was at the center of the process as you went through it."

"Why didn't you tell us?" Dr. Fagan asked.

"Because that wasn't my place. I'm Kaden's polarity, not his spokesperson. I knew when he came back, he'd explain to you, and it's his power to explain. I'm just his, his... support system," he said, finally finding the words he wanted to describe his part.

Of course, I didn't think support system even remotely explained it, but it would do for now. They didn't need to understand just how intense my love and connection to Lysander was. That was private and very intimate.

"Gedi, Gedi, Gedi." The chants were getting louder.

"What's Gedi?" I asked the group, confused about what the islanders were saying.

Elana chuckled. "Gedi is the Fire God in this region." She looked over at Lysander and winked before saying, "He's also their fertility god."

"Oh, that's appropriate," I said before I could censure myself. My full-on blush must've helped alleviate the seriousness of the situation, because they all chuckled.

"You'll need to go over there, Kaden," Lysander said. "They need to see you. I guess this group will benefit the most from what you just created. They need to be able to thank you."

I nodded and led Lysander over to the celebration.

The islanders partied for three full days and nights. Other islanders from miles around came to celebrate as well, the party growing more and more by the day. I was sure they celebrated even after we left, but even though the island-building process didn't wear me out, the parties sure did.

Lysander and I made love in a hut the islanders had decorated with flowers and seashells. Luckily, the partying kept the much more solemn specialists and experts at bay. There would be plenty of time for analysis. For now, I just wanted to be with Lysander knowing I didn't have to worry about losing control again and accidentally incinerating him.

Part Three

The Reckoning

Chapter Thirty-One

Lysander

G OING BACK TO SCHOOL after experiencing the entirety of Kaden's power was anticlimactic. The islanders treated Kaden like a god, with me as his companion. Then, when we were back on the airship, Kaden and I were put through tests and interviews over and over.

I was quicker to become irritated than Kaden and finally told them I was done with the interviews. He, however, was like the Buddha we'd seen in the dream together. He answered the same questions over and over. He did experiments when asked. Even the finer things that had given him trouble were completed with no problems. He was now truly a master of his powers *and* his patience.

"Are you okay?" I asked a few days after we returned to school, and finally had a moment to ourselves.

"Yeah, I'm great. Why?" he asked.

"You're so quiet and calm. All that tension you used to carry around is just gone."

"The volcano burned it out of me," he said, chuckling.

I kissed him. "You're snarky too, but seriously, I know they've been putting you through your paces since we got back. Are you sure it isn't getting to you?"

Kaden rolled over. "Now I know and understand what I am, Lysander, I'm finally no longer afraid. I've never not been afraid. Afraid I'd be abandoned, afraid I'd be moved to a new home, afraid of what my foster parents would do, then after I was sold, afraid every day of what the men I encountered would do to me. I'm no longer afraid, Lysander. It's like a veil has been lifted from my eyes, and I see the universe as it is. And the truth is, it's nothing to be afraid of."

"Like what? You're no longer afraid of dying, or no longer afraid 'cause you know you can kick anyone's butt that comes up against you."

Kaden's hand paused as he was sweeping it through my hair. "I don't think there is such a thing as death. Everything keeps recycling." He resumed the stroking and leaned down to kiss me. "But yeah, I'm not concerned about anyone trying to hurt me any longer, either."

He lay back on the bed and stared at the ceiling. "I guess the biggest relief is that I no longer worry about what might happen if I lose control. I will never lose control again, not as long as I have my faculties about me. That's the greatest relief of all, I think."

We stayed like that until we fell asleep. My boyfriend had always been special, but now he was even more so. Not only did he have control over his powers, not only was he the most powerful man in the world, but he was the very essence of calm and collected. That put everyone, even me, at ease.

"Do I really have to do it again?" I asked Elana, who had just told me to practice siphoning off her Fire powers.

"You know the answer to that, you've done well with my Air skills, but you still have to learn to take only small parts if you don't want to die if you ever find yourself in battle again."

I huffed and tried again. Pulling at Elana's powers and gently taking only small bits of her energy, then banking it in the earth. In Professor Sturgis's class, we learned the opposites of each power. Air would build Water and Fire, but was subdued by Earth, well, sort of. Wind was an acceleration of Air when connected with Earth. Fire was subdued by Earth and Water. Water was subdued by Earth and Fire.

So, naturally, when I pulled Elana's powers, I banked her Fire elements into the earth to contain them without extinguishing them. "Your powers are rare too, Lysander, but at least we know more about them than Kaden's."

As much as I hated the exercises, I could feel myself getting stronger by the day. More than once I zapped Kyle's telekinetic skill when he was threatening me with some of his never-ending practical jokes.

I'd only done Kaylee's powers when we were practicing, and she volunteered to let me. Everyone's powers returned within an hour or so of me absorbing them. If I stored them in the elements around me, they returned a little slower, but no one had ever been without their powers for more than two hours.

I was forbidden from ever practicing with Kaden. Even though he was my lover and my polarity. His powers were so intense if I absorbed them, even a small aspect of them, I'd be wiped away. "Just don't ever try," Elana had warned.

I couldn't imagine why I'd ever need to. It was fun to harass Kyle, but I only did it when he had it coming, and Kaden never had it coming. If anything, he was even kinder and more gentle-hearted after the island incident.

Word spread of Kaden's actions in the South Pacific, and the island was on every social media platform and every news outlet worldwide. Kaden's name was never mentioned. Instead, the media had adopted the Islander's name for him. Gedi. "So, Gedi is your superhero name, I guess."

Kaden just smiled and shrugged. "It doesn't matter to me what I'm called."

It does have a nice ring to it. "Gedi, sort of like Yeti, except you play with fire and not snow."

"Yeah, it's cool, but I don't think it fits. Building the island required all four elements. The Fire element was just one of them."

"Trust me, it was the most impressive from where we were standing," I said.

"I'm sure, but no, I don't think Gedi should be my permanent superhero name. Maybe we should give that one to Elana. She can be the Fire Goddess."

I laughed. "I'd guess if she were going to take on a fire name, she'd go with a goddess."

Kaden kissed me like he did when he was teasing or messing with me. "You're probably right."

By spring, we'd all fallen back into the routine of school. Unlike regular universities, ours didn't get a spring break. Instead, we had frequent breaks built into our schedule. In the second semester of freshman year, the different societies representing the four powers began inviting students to long weekends where they were groomed to join their society.

Often, like Kaylee and Kyle's telekinetic society, students were groomed to work in fields that enabled them to put those skills to the best use.

Kayden tended to go to the Water tribe with Dr. Fagan on these long weekends. I, however, was forced to go on tedious events with the Terrestrial society. So, that meant I was stuck with witches, were-animals, and anything considered magic.

I had so little in common with them, I would swear I often felt like the third wheel I'd been in high school. Even though they were only three-day weekends, I missed my little tribe of Kyle, Kaylee, and Kaden.

The only consolation was I could constantly zap power away from annoying assholes in the group. For some reason, Terrestrials seemed to have an overabundance of bullies. Now that I knew how to siphon off their powers and absorb them, I could zap without fear or concern—much to the dismay of several assholes I tended to get stuck with on every society weekend.

The best part was coming back to Kaden. I didn't know whether absence made the heart fonder or not. I was already about as fond of Kaden as I could be.

After months of him staying every night with me, we finally moved in together. There was no need for him to have a room to himself, especially in the hall where they'd put him. It was in one of the oldest buildings and smelled like feet and gym lockers.

Here he was with Kyle, Kaylee, and me. His friends. Well, maybe more accurately, his family.

On the spring equinox, a time when Terrestrial powers were supposedly at their most powerful, although I couldn't tell the difference, all Terrestrials were brought in to organize the equinox celebration.

We'd all just settled in to get assignments when Dr. Aynesworth, who was the head of the school's Terrestrial group since he had the terrestrial gift of healing, came into the auditorium and asked us to settle down for a moment. He looked harried, like he'd just heard the worst news.

I immediately worried it had something to do with Kaden. I'd only ever seen that expression on Dr. Aynesworth's face when he was dealing with him.

"I have a grave announcement. Dr. Grace Bisbee, former Dean of Students, has gone rogue."

The entire room erupted noisily. I didn't react, though. Instead, something about the information settled heavily in my stomach. Dr. Bisbee was the *former* dean of students because of what she'd done to me. Would it mean she'd retaliate against me? Surely not with Kaden keeping watch.

Dr. Aynesworth put his hand up to get our attention again. "She disappeared several days ago, but her coworkers said she was making plans to return here to our school. If any of you have been in touch with Dr. Bisbee, you must let us know. I don't need to tell you how powerful she is. If she is no longer a friend of this school, everyone here could be at risk."

The noise erupted again after that announcement, and Dr. Aynesworth stepped out of the room. I needed to talk to the twins and Kaden. If she'd gone rogue and had a vendetta, I was almost sure I was on top of her list of students to come after. If given another chance, I was sure she'd succeed in killing me.

I left the assembly without volunteering to help. I might be a Terrestrial, but in name only. I never felt like I fit in with them and decorating the auditorium for an event wasn't for me. In fact, it seemed more like torture than fun.

I still didn't understand. Everyone else in the Terrestrial group—be it those who called themselves fairies to those who could walk through walls—loved these events. Why did I hate being with them so much?

I shook the questions from my mind, convinced I had bigger fish to fry, as my mom always said when dealing with a conundrum.

When I entered the dorm, Kaden was sitting in the lounge with the twins, watching a soccer tournament. "Hey, guys, can you pause that a minute? I just got some, well, not great news."

Kaden took the remote and paused the game, then all three turned their attention to me. "So, Dr. Aynesworth just told the Terrestrial's party planning group that Dr. Bisbee has gone rogue. He thinks she's headed here."

"Wait, Dr. Scarypants is coming here?"

I almost chuckled at Kyle's description of Dr. Bisbee. If it hadn't been such a serious situation, I would've. Instead, I nodded. "We need a plan of action, 'cause I'm guessing if she's coming, it'll be me she's after."

The group stared at me for a long while before Kaylee shrugged. "Kaden will protect you." She reached across her brother to take the remote from Kaden's hand.

"Not necessarily. What if she does her mind-meld thing on him? Remember the lightning bolt?" I asked.

Kaylee shook her head. "That was before Kaden got control of his powers. I doubt she could handle holding that tiger by the tail," she said, pointing at Kaden.

She turned the game back on and ignored me. "Kaylee, really?" I asked, frustrated.

Kaden got up, and, taking my hand, led me back to our room. "Don't worry too much about it—Kaylee's right. I'm not the same as I was when she manipulated me back in the fall. Hell, neither are you. You stood up to her when you hadn't learned how to control your powers and lived to tell about it. Now, you could disable her easily enough."

"No, she's too powerful, Kaden. I can siphon off some of her powers, but certainly not all of them, and if she has her polarity with her, I can't overcome her skills."

"Then stick close to me. I can tell when she's needling in my mind. I can disorganize her atoms if she pushes too far."

That did cause me to laugh. "What would you put them back as?" I asked, feeling more at ease about things.

"Oh, let's see, what about a worm?"

"A worm with mind-melding skills? That sounds scary. What about a blade of grass?"

"Oh," Kaden said, "I like that. Then we can mow her when she starts getting too feisty."

Dr. Aynesworth's concerns seemed to have been unfounded. Weeks turned into months, and Bisbee never showed up. If she was targeting the school, it was unlikely anything would happen before the summer break.

Like everything else, Erudo College did graduation differently from other schools. Graduation night was a huge event, and the mountainside around the school was transformed into what looked a lot like a Greek amphitheater.

The rest of the grounds contained great tents, making the entire area look like a giant circus. Terrestrials covered the grounds with summer-like weather, although it was still snowing everywhere else along the Continental Divide where our school sat. Magic was in the air, and even I got excited by all the events, which was weird, since I tended to hate everything Terrestrial powers did.

Instead of long, boring, never-ending speeches, the event was a bonanza of acts put on by the graduating seniors. Most of Erudo's senior year students were creating their final projects. They had to display the extreme abilities they could perform without causing potential danger to the attendees.

Nosupes attended the events along with Supes. Families of the seniors were welcome and encouraged to attend whether they had powers or not. The rest of the student body was required to attend as many events as possible; not only to support the graduating seniors, but to ensure each senior had a crowd of observers to support them on their final day of school.

Kaden came over and took my hand. "You seem happy," he said as I scanned the crowds.

I laughed. "I've always been a carnival geek. I used to dream of being one of the musclemen in *Cirque du Soleil.* What?" I asked, surprised at his confused expression. "Have you never seen it?" He shook his head. "I'll show you tonight when we get back to the dorm. I think the first time I watched them perform was when I figured out I was gay."

"Okay," Kaden said, and chuckled. Oh, this would be fun. No gay man could watch the musclemen crawl over one another in those performances and not want to rip the clothes off their boyfriend afterward.

As we went through the different events, I was surprised to see people I'd eaten with, hung out with, and gotten to know, perform some of the most amazing, mind-blowing things imaginable.

Most people would be surprised to learn how little we did with our powers outside the classroom. Usually, our instructors challenged us so hard during class that we didn't have any desire to use them when we were hanging out. I guessed that was one of the good things about the school.

However, not seeing these individuals' powers meant I didn't know all they were capable of. Not until now. I ooohed and aahed as much as the Nosupes. My classmates were intensely talented, remarkable human beings.

That evening I went to bed, cuddled firmly in my space next to my boyfriend, and thought happily of how proud I was to be at Erudo College. I honestly didn't know much about the other superhero schools. But to be honest, I always figured they'd be sort of hierarchical—one power seen as greater than the other. Here, that wasn't the case. I would probably be the lowest on the totem pole at other schools.

Our second semester Basic Powers and Abilities class had focused entirely on understanding exothermic versus endothermic abilities. That was the only time I'd heard a discussion of sidekicks and superheroes.

At Erudo's, those terms were almost taboo. For that reason, my very passive endothermic abilities were regarded as just as significant as Kaden's intense Exothermic ones. That made me feel, well, equal, I guessed.

I walked through the exhibits, and yes, clearly, some students had flashier skills than others, but that didn't seem to discourage the onlookers from oohing and aahing as much for both. The entire event was a celebration of Supes, no matter what or how powerful their powers may be.

Chapter Thirty-Two

Kaden

"**S**O, CAN YOU COME?" the young woman with a strong foreign accent on the other end of the line asked me again.

"Like I said," I responded with a chuckle, "I'll ask my boyfriend. If he comes with me, I'd be happy to join you."

She squealed with delight. Not unlike earlier when she'd done the very same thing. "Miss Banuve, I'm going to have to let you go. But I'll let you know what Lysander says."

"Thank you, Gedi," she said.

Before she hung up, I added, "I'm sorry, but Gedi is the name of someone very important to your people. I don't feel comfortable with it. I'd prefer you just call me Kaden."

She paused for a moment, then said, "Okay, I will speak to my people about it."

"What was that all about?" Lysander asked when I put the phone down.

"Wanna go back to the island in the South Pacific instead of going home for break?"

"The one you helped to make?"

"Sure, if you want to put it that way. The one I helped to make."

I'd repeatedly told people I no more made the island than I made Hawaii, but no one would listen. At least Lysander now said that I helped to make it. That was easier to accept.

"Why?" Lysander asked, looking concerned.

"That was one of the Fire Elementals from that area, and the Supes around the island have been prepping it and making it habitable. They want me to come and celebrate its grand opening as a habitable island."

"Wow, that didn't take them long. I figured it would take years. Never mind, I forgot about you raising it from the depths in less than three days." I gave him the eye. "Okay, sorry, *helped* raise it from the depths. I honestly don't know why you can't just take credit where it's due."

"Because that's not what happened," I said, feeling frustrated.

Lysander put his notebook down and frowned. "That was insensitive of me. I'm sorry, Kaden. I know what you mean. I just get frustrated when you're constantly trying to explain it to people."

I let out a breath I didn't even know I was holding. "It's important to keep explaining because the Earth isn't just a thing to be dominated. Humans and Supes must start seeing the elements as sentient beings just like you and me."

Lysander got up and came over to where I stood, took my face in his hands, something he tended to do frequently, and pulled me down for a kiss. "Then we'll continue to explain. If it's important to you, it's important to me."

That caused me to smile. "So you're good with going to the island?"

"Of course. Do you think we can take Mom and Pete? I want to spend time with them this summer, and I'm guessing if we go to the island, the islanders aren't going to give up their hero, at least not easily."

"I'm sure they'll be okay with whatever. It seems important to them."

"Cool, I'll call Mom then and let her know."

Miss Banuve was ecstatic when I called back and said I was coming and bringing my boyfriend and his family with me. "Will we be staying on Crater Island?" I asked, and the woman caught her breath.

"No, of course not. You'll be staying on Ngendi Island. *Your* island."

"Oh, sorry, I haven't been back. I didn't think you could be that far along with making it habitable."

"You'll be surprised, Gedi, very surprised."

I hung up and went to warn Lysander that our accommodations might be limited since we were staying on an island that was less than six months old.

"Okay. Well, if Mom and Pete aren't happy, we can put them on Crater Island. I'm happy to stay with you wherever," he said, and kissed me before rushing back to our room to finish packing.

We had one week to spend in Denver, which was amazing. Denver in late spring was beautiful. Lots of flowers blooming on the mountainsides. We bustled around, shopping for things we could use while on the island, like snorkel equipment and fins.

I needed an entirely new wardrobe, and still without a penny to my name, I had to accept help from Lysander's mom. "Are you sure I need all this?" I asked when I looked at the new swim trunks and diving equipment. "I have a working relationship with water, so I'm not sure I'll need it to swim among the reefs."

"Stop complaining," Lysander said. "She loves shopping. In fact, she's an addict, so just roll with it."

I sighed and gave up, letting her buy whatever she wanted. I'd never had anything of my own to be concerned about, so I wasn't sure why it mattered that I had one pair of swim trunks over another. Or the suit she said I'd need for the dedication ceremony.

After the week of shopping, we packed our over-stuffed bags onto the airship and flew back to the South Pacific.

From the air, I could see the new island. The one they'd named Ngendi. Supposedly that related to the god Gedi, the name they kept using for me. I still didn't understand, not that I needed to. I was just an instrument that'd been used to create the island. I wasn't one of the people who'd be using it.

I was shocked. The island looked like it had been there for thousands of years. Extensive thick forests covered it, and even from up above, I could see areas being farmed with animals dotting the small farmsteads. It was incredible.

The moment we landed, they treated us like royalty. Libby and Pete were escorted to a beautiful bungalow next to what looked like a mini palace. I could hear the ocean lapping on the sand. Sand that hadn't been there before. Beautiful black beaches. Somehow these people had transformed the hard lump of rock I'd left here in January into this.

Miss Banuve shook off the formality and demanded we call her Ana. She showed Lysander and me around the island after she assured us that Lysander's mom and Pete were being pampered with massages and seaweed wraps. "We haven't been in touch with you much since the island was created. We were busy developing the land."

"Why so fast?" I asked, confused by the speed of the transformation.

She looked at me strangely. "Do you mean no one has told you what you have given us?"

I shook my head, and Lysander moved closer to me, sensing it was something important.

"We are the Oi Keda people. Unfortunately, because of global warming, our island is being reclaimed by the sea. Before the new island was formed, we were about to be forced to evacuate our smaller island and move somewhere like Fiji or even to the mainland. It would've ended our culture and our society forever."

"And you can use this island to migrate to," Lysander said.

"Yes, and no. Our island is less than one hundred kilometers away. The family that occupies Crater Island are relatives of ours. Eventually, yes, the smaller islands will be taken back by the sea, and all of us will have to relocate here, but for now, families will continue to occupy our ancestral land while new families colonize this one."

"That's so cool," Lysander said. "I've heard about your plight. I can understand why this is such an important transformation now."

"It's like you understood our plight and came to our rescue. Thank you, Gedi."

I smiled. The Earth didn't build the island here because of the plight of the people any more than it created the islands in this chain for the humans that occupied it. The Earth simply wanted to grow, expand, and change its landscape. Despite that, I was happy the people could use what was built.

Humans, animals, the elements, and all things were connected. That was what I learned while embodying the elements to build the island. I wondered if humans would ever understand that.

At each farm we visited, the people bowed before me like I was royalty. It was so outside reality that I struggled not to laugh. But I did understand how concerned these people must've been over losing their homes. Naturally, it would be important to them.

When we got to the far side of the island and found the small knoll where Lysander and the specialist team had been standing when the island consumed it, the area still looked untouched, like it would have if left to nature.

Ana took us to meet a group of people looking out over the landscape.

"Gedi, meet our Supe crew. They are the ones who have transformed the island into what it is today."

Most of the group were older, but two young women stood among them who were closer to our age. As I looked, I realized they were the spitting image of Ana.

"Gedi, Mr. Phillips, meet the crew." Ana introduced each of the people to me and told me what their powers were. When she got to the two women, who looked like her, she said, "These are my sisters, Ateca and Aliti."

I shook each of their hands. The group eagerly showed me how they'd transformed the earth into usable land. They joined hands, and to my surprise, all four elements came together and made the hard lava rock into usable soil. But I noticed it was limited to just the small area around them. They must have done this to whole island, just one small area at a time.

I admit my experience around decent people was limited, be they Supes or Nosupes. But I'd been around enough to know it was unusual for people to understand what caused the universe to work. I knew instantly after seeing this group interact with the elements that wasn't the case with them. It gave me hope.

The progress they were making seemed slow and tedious. I could've completed the tasks for them in less than an hour, but something about the group, the pride they showed in their work, made me think that would be rude and inconsiderate. So, I nodded to each of them and said how beautiful it was to watch them work.

Ana translated for them, and they all smiled brightly and waved at me.

"So you're a triplet?" Lysander asked Ana as we walked back toward the vehicle that'd brought us here.

She laughed. "No, not exactly. We are clones of one who died. She was a Supe, and when she knew she was dying, she split her genes into three. So, we are like triplets, but not."

I'd never heard of that, but it felt rude to ask questions. The women were important to the tribe, and from what I saw as the team worked alongside one another to make the land habitable, I assumed they were good people. The group, at the very least, would have to trust one another implicitly to create like they were. Not to mention, as we'd learned at school, the polarities would also have to be represented among the group. If time allowed, I would enjoy spending time with them and learning more.

Chapter Thirty-Three

Lysander

THE ISLANDERS WERE EXTREMELY nice, but this was Kaden's trip. Not that I could blame them. I'd watched a heart-wrenching high school science class special about how several South Pacific islanders were facing loss of their homes and communites as water levels rose, storms became more violent, and seawater temperatures rose.

The island must genuinely feel like a godsend to them.

When Ana brought us back to the palace, called the Gedi House, in honor of Kaden, I decided to hold back and let Kaden finish the tour while I hung out with Mom and Pete.

Of course, they were soaking everything up. The small bungalow they were staying in had direct access to the beach. Mom was lying on a towel, soaking up the sun, and Pete was swimming in the waves. I quickly changed into my swimming trunks, went out, and plopped down next to Mom.

"It's beautiful here, isn't it?" I asked.

"Mmm," she said.

"Okay, so the massage went well, I see."

"Beyond good. I can hardly move I'm so relaxed."

"Okay, I'll leave you alone and go harass Pete."

"That's lovely, dear," she said, and I doubted she even knew I left.

Even though I was not even remotely an expert, the waves looked perfect for surfing if we'd had a surfboard. But close to the shore where Pete was swimming, it wasn't so bad.

I dived in next to him and tried to dunk him just like he did me every time we went swimming. I came up just in time to get a face full of water.

We played until we were both tired, crawled onto the sandy beach, and sat close enough to the surf for the water to lap against our feet.

"You said Kaden created this island?" Pete asked.

"I watched him do it," I said, feeling proud of him.

"Shouldn't it be a bald spot of steaming volcanic rock?" he asked.

"It should be, and part of it still is, but the islanders have a team of Supes converting it into usable land."

Pete nodded, and we stared at the ocean for a long time.

"I don't understand all this, you know. It's outside my comprehension."

"If it helps, it's hard for me to comprehend too, or at least it was before it all happened."

Pete took a deep breath. "So, I heard someone talking while we were waiting for the massage. They said Kaden was your polarity. What is that?" he asked.

"Oh, well." I thought for a moment remembering how they described it in class. "So, you know when you have two magnets. When you turn it a certain way, it repels the other, but when you turn it around, it's attracted to the other?" He nodded. "Well, it's pretty much the same as that. Except when polarity Supes are together, they magnify the other's powers."

"So, that's what you are to Kaden?"

I smiled at him and nodded. "It's what he is for me too."

"So, all this is here because you helped him?"

I touched my finger to my nose, just like he'd always done when I got his point.

"He tried to use his powers before I came out to the island, but it didn't work. When I was with him..." I lifted my arms and moved them in a semi-circle indicating the island, "...he was able to do this."

"Damn, and I just thought he was your boyfriend."

"He's that too," I said, and lay back in the sand.

"So, this is more serious than just two people dating?" he asked, and I realized this was the point of our conversation.

"Are you asking if I'm in love with him?" Pete's face looked a little green, and I had to stifle my smile. "Um, yeah, I'm head over heels in love with him. Have been for a while now."

"Does your mom know?" he asked.

"No, not yet. We're still learning what it means to be in love, so there's no rush or hurry. Neither of us has proposed or anything."

I could see the relief on his face. I looked over to the man who'd been all but my father for the past fifteen years, and asked, "Why, Pete, what's on your mind?"

"All this, it's a lot, like a really big thing to digest. It's hard to think of you as part of something or someone who could create an island." Suddenly he looked alarmed. "Don't get me wrong, Libby and I both think Kaden is a great kid. He's definitely got your best interest at heart, and he watches you like a hawk. It's just... he's so powerful."

I reached over and patted Pete on the arm to soothe him. "I'm pretty powerful too, nothing like Kaden, but no one is as powerful as Kaden. I'm his polarity, so I'd have to be pretty powerful to be that. We're still learning the depth of what those powers are."

Pete looked over at me, and asked, "So, why are his easier to see?"

"Mine are more passive. His are something that might explode or grow an island, whereas mine are reactionary. I can absorb the powers of others and store them in the environment, like storing energy in a battery. He creates energy, and in a way, I can store it."

"So, you're like *his* battery?" Pete asked, and just like that, a lightbulb came on in my head.

I laughed. "Well, Pete, I've never thought of it that way, but yeah, I think that's exactly what I am. Or I could be if I ever figure out how to use my powers to be that."

"That's fucking cool," he said, just as Mom came up behind us.

"What's fucking cool?" she asked.

"I'll let him tell you," Pete responded, as he stood up. "I'm gonna go shower, then hopefully get something to eat. I'm starving."

That night, Kaden was paraded around the beach like the god they professed him to be. I could tell he was getting tired of all the attention. Kaden was nothing if not an introvert. I'd speak with Ana tomorrow and tell her they needed to worship him a little less, if they wanted him to last more than a few days here.

For now, I leaned back in one of the chairs someone had put out for Mom, Pete, and me to sit on while we enjoyed the festivities.

Around midnight Mom and Pete turned in, heading for the little bungalow they were staying at.

I got up and waved at Kaden when he finally turned his attention back toward me. Then I headed into the main house to our bedroom.

As soon as I got to the lanai, as the locals had called it, a woman I'd never seen before stepped out of the shadows and said Kaden had asked if I could join him up in the hills.

I smiled. Damn, my man was romantic. I nodded toward the girl. "Just let me go to the restroom, and I'll meet you back here."

"No time for that," she said, and the next thing I knew, I was being tasered. That was the last thing I remembered.

Chapter Thirty-Four

Kaden

OKAY, SO THE WHOLE thing of being worshiped was getting old, and I mean getting old fast. When Lysander waved at me, I immediately tried to get away from the dancing crowd but was quickly pulled back in. Shortly after, I felt a jolt of electricity go through me, and I immediately began worrying about him.

We finished another circle, and I raised my hand, making the fire in the firepit rise above the trees, causing everyone to drop my hands and ooh and aah.

I took that as my opportunity to rush back and check on Lysander. He was nowhere to be seen. The bedroom door was closed, and the bathroom was empty. I used my powers to create some light around the house, but I couldn't find any trace of him.

By the time Ana found me on the lanai, I was in full panic mode. "Lysander's disappeared. Would your people have taken him somewhere?" I asked.

She looked confused and shook her head. "No, everyone is at the party. Are you sure?"

"Yeah, Ana, I'm sure. He wouldn't have left without telling me where he was. We need to find him and fast!" I demanded.

She nodded and ran toward the beach. A second later, I heard a shell alarm sound.

People rushed to where I stood, and most of them were in various stages of inebriation. Shit, they weren't going to be any help.

I rushed toward where the forest touched the lanai and forced my powers back into the earth, connecting with the now sleeping spirit there.

I did the same with the Air and Fire and searched for any trace of him.

The only thing I could find, the only possible trace of him, was an airship headed toward the mainland. That must be it. I was just about to send the Air toward the ship when I heard Libby behind me. "Kaden, what's going on?"

I shook my head, trying to focus on forcing the airship back to the island. "Kaden," she demanded. "What's going on."

"Libby, damn it!" I said as the control left me, and I lost the ship.

I turned to her and could see fear in her expression. "Someone's taken Lysander. I was trying to get him back."

"Are you sure?" she asked, and I just nodded.

"Ana, I need an airship, and I need it now!" I demanded.

I could've used my powers to follow them, but I was still learning, and I had no idea who or what I was dealing with. Who would kidnap Lysander right out from under my nose?

Libby and Pete climbed aboard the ship with me, and within minutes we were in pursuit. Unfortunately, I'd lost my connection and whoever was in control of the ship had some cloaking device that masked its trail. Something the pilots argued wasn't possible unless it was new technology they weren't aware of.

When we got back to the mainland, I demanded we go directly to the school. "We'll have more resources there," I said, and the pilots radioed the school to let them know we were coming.

I couldn't console Libby and Pete. I was too busy searching, using my powers, trying to find any evidence of a cloaked airship. So, when I turned around after finally giving up, the panic on their faces made me feel guilty.

"I'm sorry, Libby, Pete. I got overwhelmed. I didn't think."

"No, son," Pete said, putting his hand on my shoulder and squeezing. "You don't have to worry about us. You find our boy. We'll be okay."

"We'll be okay when you find my Lysander," Libby said.

I nodded. "I'll find him, Mrs. Phillips, and when I do, God help whoever kidnapped him."

She nodded, her face as fierce as my resolve.

When we landed, we were met by the same guards who'd once been in charge of me. This time they tried to encourage Libby and Pete to follow them to the Nosupes building. A place outside the school for people who didn't have abilities to stay when they were there.

When they protested, I turned to the guard, and said, "He's their son. If they aren't welcome here, we'll go somewhere else."

The man was momentarily taken aback. He'd never heard me challenge him or anyone before, but things were different now. The love of my life, the very essence of my happiness, had been kidnapped. I didn't have the time or energy to deal with niceties.

"That won't be necessary," I heard Dr. Aynesworth say behind us. "They can come into the main facility. There are no students in residence at the moment."

I nodded and we followed him to his office, instinct telling me not to discuss things in public. Something was off. Something told me we were dealing with more than a simple kidnapping. My senses were also telling me this was all about me. If they were using Lysander as a pawn, he was in real danger, and spies could be anywhere."

When we got to Dr. Aynesworth's office, Libby and Pete were invited to sit at the back. Seconds later, Dr. Fagan and Elana walked in with grave expressions.

As soon as we were all seated, Dr. Aynesworth dismissed the guards. "Elana, can you raise the security wall?"

I had no idea what that was, but seconds later, a cloud of smoke circled the walls of the president's office.

"Okay, that will give us a little more privacy."

"I'm afraid the situation is more dire than you may realize," Dr. Aynesworth said. He looked over at Dr. Fagan and Elana and sighed before turning to me. "Kaden, we believe the person behind this is Dr. Grace Bisbee."

The moment he said her name, the puzzle pieces came together, and I nodded.

"Who is this Dr. Bisbee?" Libby asked.

"She is... was, our dean of students." I could tell Dr. Aynesworth was searching for the right words when Dr. Fagan stepped into the conversation.

"Have you ever heard of Vega?" he asked.

Of course, we'd all heard of Vega. Even with my limited education and background, the villain of the century's name had filtered down to my meager world.

Both Libby and Pete nodded. "Dr. Grace is her daughter."

"Wait, what?" Pete said, jumping up. "You let the world's most notorious villain work here?"

Dr. Aynesworth shook his head. "No, but we did let her daughter work here. We do not judge our applicants by their parents, sir. She was a Supe the same as anyone else and had the same rights to learn and teach here as any other."

"Except she's kidnapped my son!" Libby complained.

"Allegedly. We don't have concrete proof yet."

"Why? Why does she want Lysander?" Libby asked.

"Because of me," I said. "Am I right? She wants him to get to me."

All three nodded at the same time. "If our theory is correct and Grace kidnaped Lysander, it's probably to get to you."

"And why? What can she do with me?"

Elana, who'd been sitting silently listening to the exchange, cleared her throat. "Do you remember the story of Vega?" she asked.

"Didn't she try to nuke a city or town or something?" Pete asked.

"But do you remember why?" she asked.

Pete and Libby shook their heads. I racked my brain for the answer. We'd studied it in class, but I'd only half paid attention. Why would I ever need to learn about some dead woman? When they died, that was the end of that, right?

"Vega and Lowen were the first documented people to acquire powers," Elana began to tell the story. "The two women were friends, or had been. They were both exposed to nuclear radiation during a government experiment. Vega was not an evil person, she simply believed in equality for everyone. She and Lowen had been actively involved in human rights projects both before and after they were exposed. But the problem was, Vega was willing to go to any lengths to create more Supes."

"Was it so she could become more powerful?" Libby asked.

Elana shrugged. "That's the story, but Erudo, the founder of this school, knew both women. He said he never believed that was actually the case. In fact, his testimony on her behalf plagued him for the rest of his life. Many established Supes, including Lowen, never trusted him after that. Regardless of her intentions, Vega hatched a plan to expose her town to nuclear material. She ended up dying in the process, leaving behind a five-year-old named Grace."

"I don't get it. Basically, you are saying Dr. Bisbee is retaliating against us because of what happened to her mom?" I asked.

All three people shook their heads. "No, Grace believed in her mom's theory. That exposing people to radiation was the best way to increase super abilities."

"And I'm a bomb. I'm a fucking nuclear bomb. She wants to use me to expose people to radiation?" I asked, already knowing the answer.

Dr. Fagan sighed and leaned forward in his chair. "Kaden, we all theorized you had the ability to do what you did in the South Pacific, but when you did it, you proved you could. Your powers are so much more powerful than just creating an island. I have no doubt you could do exactly what she wishes."

"So, what do you think she's going to do, threaten Lysander if I don't comply? I'll blow her to smithereens."

"I doubt she'll care," Elana said. "I'm sure it's worth her life if it proves her mom's theory.

"How do you know all this, young lady?" Libby asked.

"I was her protégé," she admitted. "I was also her teaching assistant for over seven years."

"How do we know we can trust you?" I asked.

"Because Grace used her powers against me when you first arrived at school. She kept me away from you, away from her responsibilities to you. At the time, we thought it was due to her need for control, which seemed to increase every year. But we realized after she'd been sent away, and I told Dr. Fagan and Dr. Aynesworth what'd happened, that she was trying to get to you."

'You should've told me," I demanded, angry enough to slam my fist into the table in front of me.

"We didn't know she was that big a threat. Her polarity had abandoned her years ago, saying she was a threat to humanity. Without him, there wasn't much she could do."

"But you've changed your mind? Why?" Libby demanded.

"Because, he went missing the night before last. We're almost sure she's kidnapped him as well."

"This keeps getting better and better," Pete snapped.

"So, what do we do now? How do we get Lysander back?"

"At her full power capacity, she can hide Lysander from anyone, even you, Kaden. We'll just have to wait until she contacts us. We'll react then."

"Not going to happen. I'll search for him, and by God, I'll find him," I said as I stood to go.

Elana stood and looked me in the eye. "Kaden, you need to conserve your energy. My shield prevents her from hearing what we say, but the moment you use your powers, she'll know it. Her spies will know and tell her. She'll wait until you've exhausted yourself before she attacks. If you wait and trust us, we think she'll come here, and we can catch her in our snares."

Elana looked between Dr. Aynesworth and Dr. Fagan for confirmation, then turned back to me after they nodded their approval. "I worked with her for many years, and before that, I was her pupil. Trust me, we... I, know her weaknesses, even with her polarity. We will use everything to save Lysander. You have my word."

I glanced at Libby and Pete and felt like melting into the floor. How could I do nothing when he was out there, God only knew where, enduring who knew what kind of torture?

Did I have a choice? No, I didn't think I did, but I knew one thing for sure, I could and would do a lot of *intentional* damage. Unlike when I'd attacked the men from the trafficking situation, I would *knowingly* destroy Grace Bisbee for what she was doing to Lysander.

Chapter Thirty-Five

Lysander

I WOKE UP DAZED and immediately scanned the room, which looked like some nineteen-sixties motel room. There was light, but it was pouring in from windows high up in the wall. I was lying on a bed, there was a recliner across from me, and some man was asleep on it.

"Hello?" I asked the figure, and he moved.

As he stirred, I figured I probably should've been afraid of him, but he didn't feel dangerous. "Who are you, and where are we?" I asked.

The man reached up and rubbed his head. "I don't know. Who are you?"

"I asked you first," I demanded, concerned he could be some sort of plant to get me to talk.

"I'm Alias Johnston. How did I get here?"

"I was about to ask you the same. I think someone tasered me. My chest still hurts," I said.

"Yeah, same with me. Wait, shit. She wouldn't have done this."

"Who wouldn't have done what?"

"Grace, damn," he said, and looked over at me. "Do you know Grace Bisbee?"

I nodded. "She was my teacher."

Realization dawned on his face. "You're Lysander Phillips?"

I felt panic that he knew my name. "Yeah, how do you know me?" I asked, jumping off the bed and standing behind it, keeping it between us and bracing for a fight.

"You do not need to fear me. Grace, however, is another matter. Damn, I'm parched," he said, and looked around the room. Finding a small plastic motel cup, he unwrapped it and filled it with water from the tap.

"When I use my powers, I get thirsty. I remember now... fuck," he said, and took another drink.

"What do you remember?" I asked, still very wary of him.

"I'm an empath. I can detect and help moderate people's emotions. Grace Bisbee is my polarity."

"Shit, so you're in this with her?"

He laughed mirthlessly. "Hardly. I told her I wouldn't help her. I'm afraid you, well, more specifically, your boyfriend, Kaden, is part of some wild scheme." He shook his head. "She must've kidnapped me when I wouldn't comply." He continued shaking his head, "Damn, damn, damn, what is that woman thinking?"

"I'm sorry. I'm confused. I don't understand any of this."

The man looked at me, his eyes sad. "Sit down, young man, and let me explain from the beginning."

I still didn't trust him, but decided I might as well listen to what he had to say.

Dr. Alias Johnston was a top-level empathic counselor working for the government. Most of the time, his job was low-level, working with potential spies in the Supe community who wished to overthrow the government.

Alias met Grace when they went to school together at Erudo College. Grace later became best friends with Alias's wife, and the three had been close.

"Did you know Grace is Vega's daughter?" he asked.

"Like the supervillain, Vega?" I asked, surprised.

"Yes, but I suggest you don't say that in front of Grace. She was only five years old when her mom died, but around forty years ago, Grace became obsessed with her mom's experiments."

He shook his head again. "My wife was an elemental, containing both Earth and Water. Grace convinced her that her mother's theories weren't wrong. That her methods might've been, but the underlying belief that exposing people to radiation, or other powerful elements, would mean that more Supes would be created."

"I don't understand. Why does she want there to be more Supes?" I asked, frustrated.

"Simple. If everyone has powers, she believes you can limit prejudice."

When I looked confused, he sighed. "I'm not saying she's right, but Vega argued that because the number of Supes accounts for less than one percent of the population, at some point, the Nosupes will see us as a threat and try to destroy us."

"That's ridiculous. Supes are less of a threat to Nosupes than the other way around."

Alias shrugged. "I suspect it has more to do with her wanting to clear her mom's name than anything else. My powers don't work on Grace like they do others, but as an empath, I can see enough to know that's her underlying issue. She hates that her mom was, and still is, the most notorious supervillain of all time."

"So, what does that have to do with you and me?" I asked, wanting him to get to the part where he and I were locked in a hotel room together.

He took a long deep breath and let it out slowly. "Grace's skill, the ability to mind-meld with others, is special, intense, and doesn't work on just anyone. Some Supes just can't handle the intrusion. Elementals are particularly vulnerable."

He looked sad and stared quietly toward the tiny window, before continuing, "My wife agreed to let Grace use her powers on her mind. Grace wanted her to expose a group of Nosupes, but she was still struggling with her skills. We were all so young. Beth, my wife, had never found her polarity, so she was... well, you could say she was vulnerable. Anyway, I wasn't in on the conversation between them, so I had no idea what they had planned. Grace began the meld with Beth, and Beth's mind couldn't handle the intrusion. Had Grace pulled back, we could've removed Beth's powers, allowed her to calm, then returned them to her, and she would've been fine."

"Wait," I interrupted, "in order to cure the madness caused by Grace's power, you have to remove the other person's power?"

He nodded. "We learned that early on, when Grace accidentally exposed her meld to students in our class."

"So, what happened with Beth? I'm guessing it didn't end well."

He looked at me, the sadness completely shadowing his face. "Grace continued to push further and further into Beth's mind. Finally, it broke her. She went completely mad and lost all access to reality. She caused several earthquakes that night, and untold damage to buildings around Denver, where the lab was. By the time we removed Beth's powers, it was too late. She never recovered."

"Damn."

He nodded, then continued, "I refused to be anywhere near Grace after that, until Dr. Aynesworth asked if I would allow Grace to return to the lab last fall. She had almost killed you when she used her powers against you. Dr. Aynesworth wanted me to evaluate Grace to see if she needed to have her powers removed permanently."

"And you let her?" I asked, surprised.

"Beth had died the year before. I figured maybe it was the opportunity to allow Grace to make amends. Surely, she wouldn't still be harboring the same desires to prove her mom's ill-fated theories. When I heard what happened, it just sounded like Grace had gotten carried away, which, to be honest, was always her biggest flaw."

"That's not the case, though, is it?" I asked.

He shook his head. "No, Grace took on a new name or persona, and has begun calling herself ScapeGrace. It means villain. After evaluating her, my team and I were able to draw that information from her. So, we decided we had to remove her powers. Long story short, before we could, she mind-melded several of my team members, caused them to murder one another, then went rogue. That was in March. We've been searching for her since then."

"I take it she found you first," I said with a sigh.

"Yes, she found me, tried to convince me her side was the right side of history. When I refused to help, she must've drugged me."

"She didn't use her powers on you?" I asked.

He shook his head. "No, we can't use our powers on each other. It's how our polarity works. I'm a stronger empath with others when she's around, and I give her a stronger grip on her mind control powers. That's her theory about why Beth didn't work out, I wasn't there with her. Had I been there, she could've controlled the meld better. But she's wrong. Some minds can't be melded. My research has shown very distinct patterns in several Supes with elemental abilities. Their minds are already melded with the element they control. We believe when Grace melds with them, she interrupts that flow, causing the madness. It's too dangerous."

"She wants to control Kaden."

He nodded slowly and looked concerned. "Kaden's powers are beyond comprehension and beyond our control. If she interrupts his connection with the elements, Kaden could very well destroy the Earth, maybe even the entire solar system. We can't let her connect with him in a mind-meld."

"Shit!" I said, stomping my foot. "Why would she risk that?"

He came over and sat on the bed next to me. "She's not thinking clearly. In fact, I don't think she's thought clearly since her mom was killed. This has been building all that time. I'm afraid we weren't paying close enough attention to the signs."

"And now, Kaden comes along, the perfect bomb for her experiment."

Alias nodded.

"Then we have to escape. We have to stop it from happening."

"I know where we are," he said. "This is where the government kept Supes they deemed a threat in the seventies. There is no way out of here, Lysander. Not unless we're let out. The facility has been all but abandoned for the past decade, but I'm guessing the few guards kept here are now under her control. With my presence, she can control multiple people for an untold amount of time."

"Can't you, as an empath, block her somehow?" I asked desperately.

He laughed. "No, it doesn't work that way. She has the overt powers, and I have the passive. I can't undo what she does, only increase her ability."

"That's why she kidnapped you?" I said, clarity coming to my mind. "She needs you to influence the guards and to get to Kaden."

"Apparently," he agreed. "And, son, my thirst means she's using my powers now. And the fact that I could drink a gallon or two means she's using them a lot. That isn't good for me, you, or your boyfriend."

"Wait, how do you know so much about me and Kaden? Not even Grace knew we were together."

He smiled and patted my arm. "Did I mention I work for the government? Kaden is practically the only subject discussed in my or any other governmental office worldwide. Yeah, I know all about how you two have progressed."

"That sucks," I admitted. "I don't like my business being out there for everyone to see."

"Welcome to the world of a Supe! Sorry, I don't mean to make light of it, but that goes with the territory, son. Especially when you're the most powerful Supe in the world."

We spent the following few hours brainstorming ways to get out, but we didn't seem to have any options. Somehow, we were stuck and at the mercy of a psycho maniac apparently willing to destroy the world to get her way.

Chapter Thirty-Six

Kaden

The message came in the wee hours of the morning the following day. Libby and Pete had gone to the Nosupe housing after we had argued until there was nothing else to say. We were stuck. The villain had screwed us.

Kaden is to be at the Hoover Facility by sunrise.

That's it. That's all the letter said.

"Where's the Hoover Facility?" I asked.

Dr. Aynesworth, Elana, and Dr. Fagan all looked chagrinned. "It's where the government used to interrogate Supes they suspected as spies."

"Why isn't she afraid of me?" I asked, finally asking what I'd wanted to know all along.

"Because she has Lysander. Your polarity," Dr. Fagan said.

Then Elana added, "Your boyfriend."

"So what, she's going to threaten to hurt him, kill him? Why can't he zap her powers? He knows how to do that now."

"Not there. The place is irradiated. Teams of specialists throughout the seventies and eighties created the facility deep in the mountains to ensure Supes couldn't use their powers."

"Then how is she using hers? I don't understand any of this."

"It's complicated. We aren't privy to all the information about the Hoover Facility. Even today, the place is classified. But we do know the agents somehow maintained their powers. You can't go in there, Kaden."

"We are *not* going to leave him in her hands," I said emphatically.

"I'm not sure we have a choice. I can alert the government officials, letting them know the facility has been compromised, but I doubt they have contingencies. Hoover was created when the world was freaking out. Not only did we have the threat of nuclear war, but we had all these superpowers coming out of nowhere."

"Hoover was a place of torture. It was..." Dr. Fagan stalled as he tried to describe it.

"It wasn't a place you wanted to be," Dr. Aynesworth said.

Dr. Fagan turned to him. "I'm sorry, Clyde, I didn't think. This must be difficult..."

Dr. Aynesworth put his hand up to stop Dr. Fagan from finishing. He looked at me and sighed. "My father and mother were both tortured there. My mom died before they were done interrogating her," he said. The word interrogating came out as a slur. "My father died a few months later. That facility echoes with the cries of innocent people tortured because of unfounded fears and prejudices." He looked at Dr. Fagan and shrugged. "It doesn't surprise me that Grace would take Lysander there. Her point is clearly being made."

"What point?" I asked, confused.

"When we aren't all equal, when there are Nosupes and Supes, one will always want to destroy the other."

It was all beginning to make sense now. "So, what do we do? I won't let Lysander die."

"I think the answer is simple," Elana said and looked at the men. "Kaden needs to do what should've been done long ago. He needs to collapse the Hoover Facility and force Grace out into the open. Then, she won't be able to control us all."

"That's not necessarily true," Dr. Fagan said. "If she has her polarity with her, even if he's an unwilling participant, she can and will manipulate us all."

"So, we counteract that," I said. "We can do it just like we did the island. You can be far enough away that she can't attack you. I'll begin by bringing Lysander out of the facility. Radiation isn't a problem for me, it's part of Earth's elements. I've dealt with Uranium and Radium when we worked with the Earth Elementals."

"Don't be too sure. These are refined, Kaden. That's very different from the stuff you experienced in its natural form."

"I'm sure that's true, but still, I don't believe it'll be a problem. You being mind-controlled by Dr. Bisbee and trying to kill me while I'm doing what I'm doing, that's where the problems begin."

The three of them sat down and chatted about the plan. But we were beyond planning at this stage. As far as I was concerned, I had a plan, one I was about to put into place... with or without their help.

Chapter Thirty-Seven

Lysander

T HE EARTHQUAKE HIT THE facility, and dust drifted from the ceiling cracks. "What was that?" I asked.

"Earthquake, I imagine," Alias said.

"Isn't that strange?" I asked.

He shook his head. "It's unusual to get an earthquake in this part of Colorado, but not unheard of."

The next earthquake was stronger, and debris from the walls began to fall into the room. "Are we going to be crushed in here?" I asked, alarmed.

Alias was at the door trying to pry it open when it flew back off its hinges and away from the room.

"Damn," Alias said, looking at his hands where just a second ago he had been gripping the door handle.

Alias's face contorted like someone was trying to strangle him. I immediately knew it was Kaden. He'd come for us, well, me. He couldn't know about Alias.

I rushed over to where Alias stood grabbing at his throat, and yelled, "Kaden, no! Friend, not foe!"

The strangling immediately stopped, and an unseen force wrapped itself around Alias and me and began pulling us out of the room.

"Not so fast!" I recognized Dr. Bisbee's voice and shuddered. Here came the showdown that would probably lead to my death.

Within seconds I felt the telltale signs of Bisbee entering my mind. I immediately resisted and tried to absorb, siphon, anything to prevent her from controlling my mind again. Something was wrong, though. I couldn't absorb anything. I was completely at her mercy.

"Help me!" I yelled at Alias.

"Stop, Grace. You're not a monster, stop!"

She laughed. "Your days of telling me what to do are over, Alias. You could've helped, and we could've prevented these theatrics, but no, you were too busy holding your grudges."

"She was my wife, and you knew better. You know better now. Stop before innocent people get hurt."

All the time Alias and Grace argued we were being moved toward what I assumed was the exit.

Grace focused back on me, and seconds later I blacked out.

Chapter Thirty-Eight

Kaden

I CAUSED TREMOR AFTER tremor to rocket through the facility. The back of the building was already collapsing when I finally got Lysander and whoever he was protecting out. Unfortunately, as Lysander flew up and out the doors I had melted when this all started, I could tell he was unconscious.

Bisbee came out seconds later. "He'll die, Kaden. If I don't lift the meld, he'll die. Start obeying my orders now if you want to save him."

A voice came from the microphone Dr. Fagan had put in my ear before moving back to a safe distance. "Listen to her, son. This is when you have to use your wits. Lysander's life depends on it."

Several men came out of the facility behind Bisbee and surrounded me. I could tell by their expressions Dr. Bisbee was controlling them.

"What do you want?" I asked, hoping to figure out how to proceed if I could get her to talk.

Surely by now, your *instructors*," she said the last word like it tasted bad in her mouth, "...have told you what this is about. I simply need you to help me expose the world to the same elements that created these powers."

"And what happens to those who can't handle it? They should just die?"

"Please, what does someone who can snap his fingers and end the Earth as we know it care if a few ants die under his feet? You're a god, Kaden. Start acting like it."

The man who was still tied up next to Lysander spoke. "None of us are gods, Grace. And killing millions of people won't create more Supes. You know the science, this is evolution, not magic. Why do you keep denying that?"

Bisbee ignored him. "So what will it be, Kaden? You can destroy me, but you'll destroy Lysander as well. You can't have both," she teased.

My studies returned to me just then, and I remembered the lessons about polarities. Dr. Bisbee's powers were increased because her polarity was here. She wanted to destroy my polarity. Maybe that was the angle. Maybe that was how I could manage this.

I didn't dare remove Lysander for fear her weird mind-melding would harm him if she lost control of him. But, if her polarity was gone...

I didn't think. I used my power to place Lysander on the ground, grabbed the man I assumed was her polarity, and took him miles away to where Elana, Dr. Fagan, and Dr. Aynesworth were.

Bisbee screamed and fell to the ground. Immediately, the men who'd followed her out of the facility began to regain consciousness.

"Point your guns at her now!" I demanded.

Echoes of the destruction of the facility behind her sounded around us. "You've signed your lover's death warrant!" she screamed and ran back into the collapsing building.

I didn't wait. I threw up a bubble around her stopping her where she stood, and brought her back out.

"Wake him up!" I demanded when she stood before me. "Wake him up, or you will endure a long and very painful death."

The men turned their guns on me then, and I shrugged. "You can't kill me with bullets, gentlemen, but you can seriously piss me off. I suggest you leave now!"

"There you are," Bisbee purred. "You aren't a super-hero, you're as much a villain as I am. Let's stop this nonsense. Join me. Let's turn this planet into what it's supposed to be, a Supe's paradise."

I sent electricity through the bubble. Not enough to kill or make her pass out, but enough to cause pain.

Once again, she screamed. "Let him go!" I demanded again.

She laughed, and this time I filled the bubble with carbon dioxide. She began coughing and choking. I took it to the point where she almost passed out, then cleared the air, letting oxygen flow back in. Before she could re-cover, I heated the bubble to the point where it wouldn't kill or incinerate her like I wanted, but would cause her significant pain.

Bisbee screamed, but I no longer cared. I was once again that boy inside the house with the evil men. They needed to die. She needed to die.

"Kaden, Kaden, stop!"

It was Lysander. He stumbled toward me. "She's not worth it, stop."

I let cool air into the bubble, and Bisbee collapsed.

The rest of the underground facility collapsed in on itself, dust flying out of the doorway. I knew Lysander could protect himself against her now. Whatever hold that evil place had on him was gone.

I turned and embraced him. "Lysander, I was so afraid!"

"I know, it's okay now, I'm fine."

I held him until I felt the same tickle I'd felt the few times I'd gone into Bisbee's office. "Surely you're not trying to meld with my mind."

"Kaden, stop her!" Lysander yelled, but it was too late. Everything around me turned dark. Anger boiled through me, and I could feel my powers wrestling to be free of my control. It was like someone had turned on all the neurotransmitters in my head at once.

Power ripped through me, pain erupting in every atom in my body, then just like that, it was over. I knew my body was processing whatever Bisbee was doing to me, but I was no longer attached to the process. I was a spirit outside my body—an observer. No longer a participant.

I saw my body arch backward, beams of light racing out of my eyes, nose, mouth, and fingers.

Bisbee was laughing, at least for a moment, until my body rose up on its own, incinerating her the moment the beams touched her.

Lysander yelled. "No! Kaden, no! Come back to me. Come back."

As I watched in horror, my body turned toward him. I knew then and there that I would have to watch as my own body destroyed the most precious thing to ever matter to me.

Chapter Thirty-Nine

Lysander

Bisbee disappeared the moment the light touched her. But that was the least of my concerns. Kaden no longer had control of his powers. I watched as he became what I had to assume was some sort of supernova.

I had to stop this, or I had to try.

"You're a battery, you're a battery," I told myself twice before screaming for Kaden to stop.

He turned slowly toward me, and I prepared myself to absorb whatever came next.

Hot searing pain surrounded me the moment Kaden's light beams touched me. I focused down, willing the Earth to absorb the energy beginning to course through me. I knew if it didn't accept the powers, I'd be incinerated instantly.

The Earth complied, and the searing pain subsided. Kaden was fully focused on me now, his powers flowing through me into the Earth. I had only moments of hope before it became clear the Earth wasn't enough. Kaden was too much. I quickly reached out to the other elements. Water, Fire, and Air and began storing Kaden's energy there as well.

To my surprise, Kaden's form was no longer recognizable. He was an orb of light, like a mini sun. I realized then even all the elements of the Earth weren't enough to hold Kaden's power.

I was forced to thrust my consciousness out elsewhere, anything in our existence where I could funnel more of his energy. The orb was growing, and I had to react quickly, so I reached out to the sun, moon, or anything close to me in the solar system.

The light in the orb dimmed, but only fractionally. Fuck, what the hell is he? I wondered.

The light became brighter, and I knew I would not survive. Kaden was more than the Earth could handle. More than our solar system could handle.

I was beginning to panic. Then it was as if I could sense a different part of Kaden. His consciousness had somehow reached out to me.

That was enough for me. I could die if he was here with me. So, I allowed myself to be at peace. As soon as I stopped controlling where or what absorbed Kaden's energy, I felt my consciousness flow out into the universe, then into the multiverse. Black holes, pulsars, stars beginning their lives with bright explosions, stars dying... destruction and life.

I looked at Kaden's body, and the light had changed. He no longer glowed with light but darkness, just like his aura had when I first met him.

I stared at him in shock. I wasn't particularly knowl-edgeable about the universe, but I had watched enough programs about space. As I faced the man I'd come to love more than any other person, I knew what he really was. With that realization came our salvation.

I turned away from the things within the universe and allowed Kaden's energy to be stored in the other. The darkness that drove the universe itself. The dark matter.

Instantly, I was disembodied. My atoms and molecules exploded and dispersed into the ether. Somehow I was still connected to Kaden, but not physically or mentally, more sub-physical. Something I didn't think humans would ever really understand.

Everything connected, yet everything apart. I knew Kaden's energy had been disbursed. It no longer resided in this one human form. In a way, I didn't think it was ever meant to. Kaden was an anomaly.

At that moment, I realized it was equally true for me. Balance must exist, even in the dark universe. There must be Yin with Yang.

Kaden was the very essence of energy, and I was his vessel by which that energy could be distributed. I wasn't a battery, that was wrong. I had been his conduit.

As if going to sleep, darkness seeped into my con-sciousness, and then I was no more.

Chapter Forty

Kaden

I REGAINED CONSCIOUSNESS LYING in a hospital bed. Every ounce of hope and happiness had been ripped from me. Even years ago, when things were at their worst, lying on hard, dirty, broken concrete, waiting for the next man to come in and do unspeakable things to me, I'd never felt this hopeless.

Dr. Fagan, Elana, and even Dr. Aynesworth came to see me. They explained what I already knew. Lysander was gone.

I remembered watching as my powers engulfed him, and he struggled with where to store them. I thought he was going to die, so I came to him and placed my hand on his shoulder.

I knew he'd felt it because he lay back, and I could see the powers around my body begin to fade, then slowly disappear altogether.

My mind was drawn back to my body as I saw his disintegrate. I knew then Lysander was no more, not just no more a part of the universe, but he had been fully and utterly absorbed.

I didn't try to use my powers since I knew they weren't there. I was empty in that way too. I'd hated those powers, convinced they were the bane of my existence, but now they were gone... I was empty.

The months I was held and questioned seemed to flow together into endless darkness and depression. At some point, a nurse asked me if I'd like to speak to someone, and I shook my head. There was nothing left to speak about. There was nothing left to live for... but there was also nothing to die for.

They gave me drugs I recognized from my childhood when tranquilizers were used to subdue me when I was angry or upset. Drugs had never worked on me before, not even when I was really young.

Now, they made me drowsy and caused me to fall asleep. I guessed the powers I'd always had prevented the drugs from working. At least now, I might be able to use them to die if that was what I ultimately decided to do.

Once the doctor assigned to me deemed me healthy enough to stand trial, I found myself sitting in front of a panel of three ancient people. Mostly, I sat there listening to them debate my life and fate as if I weren't there.

"He is powerless. He's the same as any Nosupe at this point," one of the women said.

"Which," the man pointed out, "...puts into debate whether we even have the power to pass judgment on him."

"Hank, that was proven in Reliance versus DeMond University. Even if a Supe's powers have been removed or, in this case, expended, we have jurisdiction if the incident occurred when the individual had their powers."

The older man nodded, clearly satisfied with the answer.

The woman who responded, with crimson dyed hair that stood up on her head as if she'd just been struck by lightning, continued. "Whether or not he has his powers now is not relevant. It's possible, if not probable, that he will regain them at any moment. The boy Lysander's powers never kept the recipient from getting their powers back. The debate we should be having is whether we should take advantage of this opportunity and dispatch the boy now while we can."

The woman who'd started the hearing, the one with grey hair, shook her head. "Russian intelligence tells us they once dispatched three young men. They were trying to prevent them from growing up with three different connections to the elements and each time, the three were born again. Not once, but twice. Even if we become evil enough to kill an innocent man for something he had no control over," the grey-haired woman looked the red-haired woman in the eye, "...he will simply be born in a different body and form. That puts us at even greater risk."

The woman pointed at me. "At least we know Mr. Pierce has made an effort each time he's been confronted with his powers to do the right thing. The ethics he has shown indicate we are better off accepting him as who and what he is."

I'd been interested in the debate when they discussed situations like the Russians. So, was that reincarnation, or were they talking about the powers showing back up? I would never find out, at least not from these three. They droned on and on for weeks.

Often they debated the very same arguments they had just a few days before. If I'd had my powers, I would've assumed they were trying to drive me insane to see if I'd blow them and myself up.

Finally, after a long time listening to them debate, I was shocked to hear them ask that I rise to face them. The red-haired woman stood, and said, "Kaden Pierce, you've been found without fault for the incidents regarding the collapse of the Hoover Facility and the deaths of Dr. Grace Bisbee and Lysander Phillips. You are free to go."

The three judges literally disappeared like magic. Two large doors opened in the back of the building, and just like that, I was free. I was also homeless, penniless, and had no one and nothing to go home to.

I thought it might have been better for them to have killed me. I strode down the busy street, trying to figure out where I was. When I'd walked no more than a block, I saw two familiar figures step around the corner. "Kaden!" Elana yelled and ran toward me, grabbing me into a hug. When Dr. Fagan caught up to me, he embraced me as well.

"I'm so sorry about all that. The ethical panel and judges have a very strict way of handling cases like this. You're lucky, though. Yours only lasted five weeks. I've known some that lasted years."

I groaned. "At least if they'd decided to kill me, that would've felt like a relief."

Elana and Dr. Fagan groaned, probably because killing me had really been on the table.

"So, what now?" I asked.

"Lysander's family have offered to take you in."

"What?" I asked, shocked. "What do you mean? I killed their son."

"No," Dr. Fagan shook his head. "No, you didn't. Grace Bisbee killed Lysander. Can't you see that, Kaden?" he asked.

Emotions welled up inside me, and I bent down on the sidewalk and wailed. "I can't live without him," I cried.

Elana and Dr. Fagan pulled me into their arms and held me as I cried. We must've stood there for over half an hour, all the emotions I'd avoided, stored away, or dismissed came to the surface as I faced the fact I was without the only person who'd ever cared for me... the only person who'd never left me. The only person I'd ever loved.

Eventually, I calmed down enough for Dr. Fagan and Elana to take me to a local restaurant, where they ordered me a hamburger and fries.

I wasn't hungry. I wasn't anything. I was absolutely and utterly nothing inside—a shell.

They ate as I picked at my food. Finally, they agreed to take me to stay at the Nosupe facility at the school. "You can stay there while we figure out how best to help you," Elana said.

"Won't Dr. Aynesworth complain?" I asked.

"No, son, Dr. Aynesworth was so relieved by your destruction of the Hoover Facility he took a sabbatical. He and his siblings are celebrating the end of an ugly time in their lives."

"So, who's the president?" I asked.

"Well, me, of course," Dr. Fagan said, smiling. "And Elana is our new dean of students."

I sighed. "Thank you, but I don't think..."

Elana put her hand on mine. "We know, honey, we know."

Most nights, either Elana or Dr. Fagan would sit with me in the room, or sometimes they both came and brought dinner. I'd refused to see Lysander's mom and Pete. I wouldn't even let the twins visit. I was beginning to believe that Lysander's death couldn't be blamed on me, but I wasn't convinced yet. The guilt was still unbearable, not to mention the grief. Seeing the friends we shared, or God help me, his parents, would break me, and this time I wouldn't come back.

Christmas was around the corner. I'd begun downloading books from the library and reading up on the Supes. For months I'd just languished. Even without my powers, I decided I could be of some use to the Supes' movement, even if I just became a vessel of understanding.

I studied the panel who'd judged me, and was surprised to learn that they had all been dead for at least twenty years. They were all Terrestrials, and before they died, they'd had their consciousnesses downloaded into a mainframe computer. That was why they disappeared after they'd rendered their judgments. I wondered why no one had told me that before.

I read and learned more about Erudo and his school, and realized I'd been brought here on purpose. It was the school of last resort. They took in the students other schools turned away. They also had some of the most well-known and well-regarded superheroes as graduates, but I guessed a school that served the weirdos would.

Christmas came and went, then the anniversary of the night the elements had used me to make the island. That was the night Lysander and I had confessed our love for one another.

I lay in my bed and cried, overcome by the loss. How could so much loss have occurred in the short span of a year?

As I lay there, I remembered what we'd been to one another. The power we had developed, not independently, but as a couple. I let my love for him wash over me, filling me once again with hope, even if it was only momentary, remembering the time I'd loved him, and he'd loved me.

I fell asleep thinking of my love for him for the first time since he'd died. On the anniversary of our love's confession, I could only think of how much I loved him and how incredible he'd been.

There was no space for anger, sadness, guilt, or grief, not when Lysander was in my heart.

As I drifted in and out of consciousness, I envisioned Lysander in my mind's eye. He was smiling and had an expression on his face that caused me to chuckle. It was the look he gave me often when I hadn't figured something out that was obvious. I called it his duh face.

"*So, you're done wallowing?*" he asked when he got close to me.

"Huh? Wallowing? I'm not wallowing."

Lysander gently kissed my lips, then pulled back. "*You are the king of wallowing. I should have the crystal you gave me for Christmas last year turned into your head so you can see yourself as the king of wallowing you are.*"

I smiled. "I miss you. I miss you so much, Lysander."

"*Well, stop. You finally let me come back. You can stop missing me now.*"

I felt a tear drip from my eye, and even though I knew I had to be dreaming, the tears felt real.

"For real, Lysander, I miss you for real."

"Open your eyes," Lysander said, and it sounded like he was really in the room. I immediately jerked my eyes open and was shocked to see him sitting on the bed in front of me.

I jumped up, then a couple of seconds later, reached out and grabbed him, pulling him into my arms.

"You're here. You're really here."

"Yeah, I've been here for, like, months, but you're so ridiculously stubborn you wouldn't let me... hell, you wouldn't let anyone in. I take it back, you aren't the king of wallowing, you're the king of stubborn wallowing."

I laughed and pulled him back into my embrace before I leaned in and kissed him.

"H-how?" I asked.

Lysander put his hand against my face and used his finger to wipe a tear that slid from my eyes.

"Honey, did you ever see me die? Did you see my body?" I shook my head. "Usually, when people die, there's something left. Even with Bisbee, there were ashes. I never died. I just stopped being in corporeal form."

I must have still looked confused, and he smiled, probably getting an idea of how to explain. "Do you remember when you evaporated on the island, you became the elements around you?" I nodded and waited for him to continue. "That's what happened with me. I could've reformed any time, but unlike you, I couldn't until you *let* me."

"I don't understand, but damn, I don't care. If you're here, that's all that matters."

He laughed. "I'm here, but... so are your powers. We have a lot of work to do. We know what we are now, or you will soon. There's a reason for us to be here, Kaden, and we've got to find out what that is."

I wiped at another tear and smiled. "Do we have to figure it out right now?"

Lysander looked at me strangely and shook his head. "No, not *right* now. Why?"

"This is why," I said, pulling his shirt over the top of his head and kissing his neck.

"Oh, yeah, that's a good reason," Lysander squeaked, and I was glad to see I still had that kind of influence on him. I had no idea why or how he'd come back to me, but now that he had, I wasn't going to waste any time worrying about destinies, fates, or shit like that.

The next day Lysander rolled over, smiling at me. "Before we get up, I wanted to tell you I think I found your name."

"What?" I asked dumbfounded, and still disoriented that Lysander was alive and with me.

"I think I figured out your best name. Potentia."

I cocked my eyebrow, making Lysander chuckle. "Seriously, I had a lot of time to think and explore while waiting for you to stop being stubborn. Potentia is Latin for power, but it's also the root word for potential. Both of those describe you, Kaden. You are powerful and full of potential. So, what do you think?"

I laughed and pulled Lysander into my embrace. "I think you're amazing, and I'm happy with whatever you want to call me as long as I have you in my arms."

Lysander kissed me. "I... um... have a name for us too. The two of us as a couple, a pair."

I looked at him, my heart bursting with love. "And what would that be?" I asked.

"Emergence. We are an emergence of power and love."

I kissed him again. "Whatever you want to call us is fine with me."

And it was, as the world finally tilted back on its axis, I realized right now, the only thing that mattered was that Lysander was back in my arms, back in my life, and I intended to take full advantage of that!

If you enjoyed Emergence, please take the time to leave a brief review at:

https://blakeallwood.com/booklink/3336362

Cursed to never find love, Crea is shocked when he finds the perfect man. Choosing to fight the curse could cost him everything, including his life.

Read **The Witch Brothers Saga,**
starting with ***Emerald Earth***

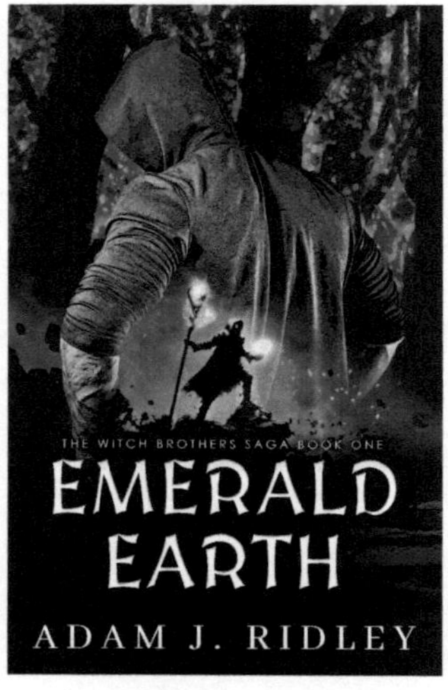

Available at your favorite bookseller!

Join Adam's email list to get advance notice of new books and receive his occasional newsletter:

www.adamjridley.com

MM Romance
By Blake Allwood

Transitions Series
Aiden Inspired
Suzie Empowered (MF Romance)
Bobby Transformed

Chance Series
Love By Chance
Another Chance With Love
Taking A Chance For Love

Romantic Series
Romantic Renovations (1)
Romantic Rescue (2)
Romantic Recon (3)

Melody Series
Melody of the Heart
Melody of the Snow

Road to Rocktoberfest Anthology
Changing His Tune - 2022

Coming Home Series (2023)
A Long Way Home
Family Home
Discovering Home
Finding Home
Bound For Home
…and many more

Novellas
Tenacious
Moon's Place

Romantic Fantasy
By Adam J. Ridley

Big Bend Series
Love's Legacy (1)
Love's Heirloom (2)
Love's Bequest (3)

The Witch Brothers Series
Emerald Earth (1)
Diamond Air (2)
Ruby Fire (3)
Sapphire Water (4)

Adam J. Ridley was born in west Tennessee, then moved to Kansas City MO after earning a degree in Early Childhood Education from Graceland College in Lamoni, Iowa. He met his husband Shaun in 1995 and they officially married in 2015, once gay marriage was legalized; although they still consider Valentines Day 1995 as their true "anniversary date". Twenty-two years later (2017), after fostering 12 children together, he and his husband sold their home, purchased an RV and began traveling the country with their two dogs.

Typically, Adam can be found relaxing in the RV or by the fire with his laptop and their Jack Russell Terrier, Buddy, curled up between his legs demanding attention. Denver, their Siberian Husky mix is often asleep at his feet or playing tug of war with Blake's husband.

Most of Adam's stories are inspired by the places they have visited in their ongoing travels. Adam's first series was The Big Bend Series, based in the area around Big

Bend National Park in Texas, his second series, The Witch Brothers Saga, occurs in the Pacific Northwest.

Adam also writes under the pen name of Blake Allwood for his MM Romance fans. His first book, ***Aiden Inspired***, was released in 2019. In 2023 he is releasing the ***Coming Home*** series which is comprised of ten-plus sweet contemporary romance novels that are based on a fictional town in his home state of Tennessee.

bibliopride.com

Books by LGBTQ+ authors